I0673757

THE ROGUE AGENT

A Scott Stiletto Thriller 8

BRIAN DRAKE

WOLFPACK
PUBLISHING
— EST 2013 —

WOLFPACK
PUBLISHING
— EST 2013 —

Paperback Edition
Copyright © 2020 Brian Drake

Published in the United States by Wolfpack Publishing, Las Vegas

Wolfpack Publishing
6032 Wheat Penny Avenue
Las Vegas, NV 89122

wolfpackpublishing.com

Paperback ISBN 978-1-64734-871-7
eBook ISBN 978-1-64734-870-0

THE ROGUE AGENT

CHAPTER ONE

Sergei Vasilov of the Russian SVR, standing at the front window of a closed shop in Berlin, peeked through blinds at a dark street.

"Where is he?" the Russian agent said. The earpiece in his ear connected him to the rest of his field team.

"There's a van turning the corner. You'll see it on your right."

He turned his head in the indicated direction, but the building wall outside blocked part of the street view.

He turned back to the storefront across the street where the exchange would take place. The target, Sallig Mahfi, owned the building. It was his playground, and Vasilov wanted to push him off the swing.

Sergei Vasilov was the kind of agent who didn't think he needed an army to kill one man. He preferred to work alone, but he had two other agents with him on this job to keep the bases covered—a team of three to kill one deadly scientist who sold home-brewed chemical weapons.

Sallig Mahfi was a former ISIS scientist. He'd survived the Russians' first attempt on his life to keep him from selling to Chechen insurgents who wanted to gas Moscow, but the resulting wounds paralyzed him from the waist down and put him in a wheelchair.

After months in hiding, Mahfi was once again in operation. His brain still worked. He still had a vast knowledge of chemistry. He still knew how to build weapons meant only for wholesale slaughter.

Moscow still wanted him dead.

For sale tonight, he had two canisters of one such home-brewed chemical agent. The Kremlin didn't think such weapons should be on the loose any more than Western Intelligence did, so Vasilov and his team had been tasked with the recovery. Moscow wanted the chemical weapon brought back for analysis.

Vasilov wasn't quite sure that was a good idea, but his superiors were genuinely curious about what Mahfi had concocted in his basement. Vasilov's concern was that Moscow might add it to the military's inventory instead of properly destroying the chemical agent.

Neither Russia nor the West was supposed to have chemical weapons any longer, thanks to various treaties that were decades old. However, if Moscow accidentally found one in the wild and managed to hide it where nobody knew it existed, it would want such a weapon not only off the books but also standing by for future use.

The only thing that ever changed in Russia, Vasilov

often thought, were the names of the people in charge.

Either way, Vasilov's orders were clear: kill Mahfi and recover the chemical weapon.

Vasilov had other ideas. Had he been solo, he could have implemented those ideas much more easily.

He'd have to improvise a little to accomplish his goal.

The tip on tonight's sale came from an informant Vasilov had cultivated in the jihadist underground for the last six months. He'd begun to fear the little man with the sugar cookie habit would never provide any useful information. That opinion had changed three nights ago when the man called in the middle of dinner and told Vasilov about Mahfi's first appearance since getting shot in the back.

Finally, Vasilov spotted the van.

"Visual on van," he reported.

"Copy."

The white panel van was equipped with a ramp to allow Mahfi easy access in and out of the vehicle. His security crew traveled up front. The van passed the storefront across the street and turned into a neighboring alley, quickly vanishing in the shadow between the buildings.

"Sedan approaching from opposite direction."

"The buyer?" Vasilov said.

"Most likely."

"Everybody in position," Vasilov ordered. He checked the autoloading pistol beneath his left arm. Round chambered, safety off, no suppressor. It wouldn't matter who heard the shots tonight.

The sedan arrived, stopping for a moment before the driver turned into the dark alley behind the white van.

Vasilov left the window and hurried to the back room, where a ladder led to an opening in the ceiling.

He climbed into the dark attic. His eyes needed a minute to adjust, but his ears picked up where his two teammates waited.

He hurried to the pair at the center of the attic. Above them was an open hatch; one of his men climbed up to the roof, and the other prepared to follow. Vasilov breathed heavily as he stopped. They were younger than him, better able to carry out the kind of derring-do the Motherland required, but he could still keep up. He could even outrun the young bucks when required.

He followed the second man to the roof. The zip-line over the street connected their building to the target location, and the line looked taut.

Vasilov glanced at his teammates. Ian Kharitonov was a shaggy-haired operator with a shooting eye sharper than anyone Vasilov had ever met. The man surpassed even *his* skills with a pistol or rifle. He was also the tallest of the group. His weapon of choice for the evening was a compact submachine gun, a Heckler & Koch MP-7.

The other, Artur Bazin, was slighter than Kharitonov but wiry and very strong. He and Vasilov carried nine-millimeter high-capacity SIG-Sauer handguns.

All three SVR agents faced the zip-line. The roof on

which they stood was higher than the one they would slide to, so the line's natural decline would help propel them across. Quickly, Kharitonov and Bazin pulled on their harnesses and hooked onto the line. Vasilov followed suit, already feeling butterflies in his stomach.

He understood that entering through the roof, where security was lax and they had already rigged an entry point, was the best way to get into the target building. What he didn't like was that it was a long way down if the harness failed.

There were some things Vasilov hated, like heights, but the Motherland was counting on him. All he had to do was not look down.

Morgan Lane, an arms dealer based in Austria, exited the sedan only when her two bodyguards gave her a hand signal that meant all-clear. The driver remained in the car. The arms dealer exited the Bentley carefully and gently closed the door.

She wore black for the meeting, turtleneck, slacks, and running shoes. Her black hair was tied back and she wore no makeup, the exact opposite of her normally exquisite appearance. When she wasn't meeting wheelchair-bound former ISIS scientists selling chemical weapons, she operated a casino resort as a front for a money-laundering operation. Her clients spanned the globe.

Morgan Lane's two bodyguards were twins, both with

slicked-back black hair, hawk-like noses, sharp eyes, and thin faces and necks. They both wore blue suits with their sports coats unbuttoned to allow room for the Glock-18 automatic pistols under their left arms.

A door opened. A swarthy man with a long beard, who was wearing a dark suit, beckoned them inside. He didn't make it obvious that he held a stubby AKS-74U "Krinkov" at his hip, but he didn't hide the weapon either.

Morgan Lane and the twins stood to one side as the man stepped ahead of them, leading the way through a storage room into the front of the closed shop. There were boxes stacked against the walls and various odds and ends lying about, giving Morgan Lane the impression that Sallig Mahfi used this location as a catch-all for junk between clandestine meetings.

She gazed at the scientist in the wheelchair as he examined her and her bodyguards. Neither spoke for a moment. Morgan's eyes moved to the large black plastic case that stood upright near Mahfi's wheelchair. It was taller than Mahfi, but not as tall as her.

"Welcome, Miss Lane," Mahfi said.

He was a touch over forty, with a scarred face. His upper body looked well-developed, but his legs were skinny and useless as he sat in the chair. He didn't cover them with a blanket.

"Mr. Mahfi," the woman said.

Mahfi's left hand moved to the black plastic case, and he patted it lovingly.

"Your weapon is here." He snapped his fingers. The swarthy man, who appeared to be Mahfi's only security even though Lane kept looking around for anybody hidden among the junk, snapped into action. He tipped the case over carefully, placing it on its bottom, then snapped open the locks and lifted the lid. He stepped back with a gesture to signal to Morgan Lane that this was her opportunity to examine the goods.

The twins tensed as Morgan Lane left them and knelt before the case. She touched the foam-packed cylindrical stainless-steel container, seeing her reflection in the polished steel, and examined the caps at the end of each canister that protected them from instant death.

She stood and said, "I suppose I have to take your word that the gas is inside?"

Mahfi rotated his wheelchair to face her. He said, "Is my reputation worth nothing? The only people who have tried to kill me are the ones who want me to stop creating my art."

"You're a death artist?"

"As are you."

Lane only nodded. From the back pocket of her jeans, she removed a cell phone. She punched in a set of numbers and showed the glowing display to Mahfi.

"As we agreed."

Mahfi nodded.

"If you'd do the honors and press the green button, the money will be moved to your account within three minutes."

Mahfi tapped the button. A green bar moved from left to right, indicating the transfer was in progress. Morgan stepped back from the case. One of the twins came forward to close the case and lift one end, while the second bodyguard took the other end. They made their way out to the car.

The cell phone pinged. Morgan Lane showed Mahfi the display.

"Not bad for a day's work," she said.

Mahfi cracked a sad smile.

Then a bullet split his forehead.

The three Russian agents zipped across the street swiftly, touching down on the roof opposite and disengaging from the line. Vasilov stepped carefully along the flat roof to a trap door. He and Kharitonov had previously inspected the insertion point and lubricated the trap's hinges to avoid any noise as they lifted the door. It made no noise now.

A ladder led to the building's second floor. Vasilov stepped through the gap, Kharitonov covering him with his MP-7. Bazin stood ready to follow.

Vasilov touched down on the floor below. Bazin hurried down the ladder next, drawing his SIG as he stepped away, and, lastly, Kharitonov joined them. The tall agent kept the MP-7 at the ready. The room was another storage area, with a narrow path to the door that opened onto a walkway overlooking the main floor. Vasilov slipped out, staying close to the wall as his teammates joined him.

The conversation below drifted their way—deal in progress. The walkway offered a perfect view of the activity below. Vasilov saw the woman examining stainless-steel canisters.

Vasilov watched, his gaze fixed. His mind raced. If he let the canisters leave with the buyers, they could kill Mahfi and accomplish half the mission.

He didn't want Moscow getting its hands on the weapon. He'd rather see it carried away and later inform the Americans than give his government another means of mass destruction.

He had Kharitonov and Bazin to think about as well. They were aware of their orders. They'd want to know why Vasilov had refused to obey. They would cause trouble for him back home by shooting their mouths off to the section chief.

Kharitonov nudged him with an elbow, an exclamation point to his thoughts. Vasilov ignored the man. Another nudge. Vasilov held up a hand, aware of Kharitonov's glare. Bazin probably also wondered why they were waiting, when the prize was in full view below.

As the transaction continued, Vasilov raised the SIG and sighted on Mahfi's forehead.

The twins in the blue suits carried out the case.

Vasilov fired once.

As Mahfi's head snapped back, the woman and the

swarthy man looked in the direction of the shot, but only for a moment. As the man below brought up the Krinkov, Vasilov and Bazin fired together. Mahfi's security guard dropped as slugs punched through his chest.

Kharitonov's MP-7 cracked, but the woman was already on the run.

The tall agent shouted an obscenity at Vasilov as he ran back into the room they'd entered from. He was going to try to shoot the buyers from the roof. Bazin shouted something as well, and Vasilov shot the thin man in the face. He started running after Kharitonov before the other man's body hit the floor.

Vasilov took aim as he entered the room, but Kharitonov's feet were already disappearing through the hatch. A car engine roared outside. The cracks of the MP-7 reached Vasilov's ears as he rose through the trap door, sighted on Kharitonov's back, and fired twice.

Kharitonov tipped forward and fell over the side, landing with a dull thud on the concrete below.

Vasilov ran to the edge of the roof. The sedan that had brought the buyers burned rubber as the driver made a sharp right turn and left the scene. They were getting away with the home-made chemical weapon.

Vasilov put his gun away and jumped into his harness once again. The downward angle of the zip-line was now a hindrance, as he had to pull himself back along the line hand-over-hand, not looking down, making terribly slow progress, it seemed, his heart racing and sweat coating his face and neck, until he reached the opposite side once again.

Still catching his breath as he drove away, the windows down to force cold air into the car, Vasilov wiped the sweat from his face.

He'd hated to kill his men, but letting Kharitonov and Bazin live meant not being able to tell Moscow *his* version of what happened. The younger generation represented by Kharitonov and Bazin, indoctrinated from a young age to obey the state, didn't have Vasilov's experience. They didn't understand the manipulations of their superiors.

They had no idea what the Motherland was truly capable of.

Vasilov knew. He was old enough to remember the old ways, which had never gone out of style.

The old ways had to end.

The dead man found by police in the smelly alley in downtown San Francisco, California, didn't mean anything to the cops.

He was simply another victim. He'd probably died in the course of a robbery, although responding officers were surprised to find his wallet and hotel key card still on him. They knew for sure he had been shot twice, once in the neck, and again through the head. The bullet wounds were not the type they generally saw in a random shooting, which were usually centered in the upper body. The head wound was especially disconcerting. The careful placement of a bullet meant the kill was personal. Powder burns on the edge of the entry wound indicated a close-range shot.

His identification said his name was William Strong of Manassas, Virginia. That didn't mean anything to the cops, either, although a dead tourist certainly wasn't something the fine city of San Francisco needed. It had enough trouble with rampant homeless defecating in the streets, which *was* driving away the tourist and con-vention business the city desperately needed to fill its constant budget gaps. The news reports of this particular death would be muted indeed.

While the morgue was processing the body and notified next of kin, word reached certain officials in Washington, DC, who took the opposite view of William Strong's death. To them, William Strong was very important. Important enough to wake up the director of the Central Intelligence Agency with the news, and also to spread the word through channels that one of their own had died under mysterious circumstances and perhaps somebody should look into the matter before any Agency activity was exposed to the public.

Scott Stiletto only had one thought as he watched the two big men follow a young blonde woman.

Can you not get yourself into trouble on vacation?

He'd come to Miami for some much-needed rest and recreation. He didn't like being on boats, but he liked the beach and found tranquility in the sound of crashing waves. Miami had plenty of beaches, plenty of places where a tired man could recuperate, and the last three days had been pure bliss.

Scott had let his mind wander, unwinding from the past several months of action and trauma. He felt like a normal human again.

It had been hard not to notice the short-haired blonde in the hotel bar over the last several nights. She wore too much makeup, which formed a mask over her face, but she had a big smile and equally big blue eyes.

She had caught Scott's attention, not only because of her attractive features, but also because Stiletto, getting older and still single, wondered if he'd ever have another companion like he'd had in his late wife, Maddy. The thought crossed his mind often when he saw women out alone, but he never acted on it.

He'd known his share of women since Maddy's death, but none of the connections had lasted long. Stiletto didn't like to think about why, forcing those thoughts away when they appeared and throwing himself into work. To forget. To run. To answer the "why" meant being honest with himself, and he wasn't ready for that.

The blonde did have a companion, however, or at least, she seemed to. He was a nervous dark-haired man, and they spoke in hushed tones with stoic faces at the bar.

They weren't lovers. There had been no personal contact between them. Stiletto recognized people in crisis. They were dealing with something big.

He had passed it off as normal human drama until the thugs appeared. Two burly men had followed the blonde as she finished her coffee shop lunch and started across the lobby to the elevators.

Stiletto followed the thugs. He carried no weapons, his personal pistol stored in his hotel room safe, but that didn't mean he was any less lethal.

The thugs had bad intentions and no mistake.

They were big men, especially across the shoulders, and each had rough hands. His first guess was the obvious one—Mafia. Miami's crime syndicates were currently thriving, according to the intelligence crossing Scott's desk at headquarters. But why target the woman?

Stiletto had been a top man at the CIA before his career ended after an unauthorized mission into Russia. Now he worked for The Trust, an organization of former intelligence officers who'd assembled operatives from all over the world for special assignments. Their mission was to defend the free world without the red tape official Western intelligence dealt with.

Scott, with a personal code of defending those without a champion, couldn't turn away from the crisis he had stumbled onto. He would know soon enough if what he'd discovered in Miami deserved the attention of the Trust.

If it didn't, he wouldn't mind spending the rest of his

vacation dealing with the problem off the books.

The elevator doors slid open, and the blonde stepped inside. One of the thugs called for her to hold the elevator. She did, and they stepped aboard. Scott jogged the remaining steps. She held the door for him too. He gave her a rushed "Thanks" as he pretended to catch his breath.

The thugs didn't look at her. She didn't look at them. She didn't look at Scott either. Her face indicated a mind deep in thought.

Stiletto examined glanced at the thugs, who had rough faces and empty eyes—the eyes of killers. They were bigger than Scott, too. He'd have his work cut out for him if the fight turned dirty.

He had to give them a little room, though. They would have to attack before he could intervene; otherwise, he'd have a lot of explaining to do to the cops and his boss.

The elevator climbed through the lower floors, past ten, past eleven, and stopped on twelve.

The doors slid open, and the woman stepped off first. Scott followed her. The thugs lagged behind, but he heard their heavy feet hit the floor before the doors slid closed.

The woman turned right down the hallway. Stiletto turned left. He stepped into the nearby alcove containing the ice and vending machines. Pressing his back to the wall, he listened. Down the hall, a door opened.

Then the woman screamed, her cry cut off sharply.

Stiletto bolted from the alcove, hurrying down the hall. The audible struggle behind the woman's door guided him to the room, where the door had been pushed against the frame but not fully closed. He shoved it open.

One thug had the woman in a headlock. He was turning her toward the other, who held a hypodermic needle in his right hand.

They were either knocking her out for a trip elsewhere or planning to inject her with a drug that would leave her dead on the floor.

The thug holding the struggling woman shouted in alarm. The second thug turned, and Stiletto delivered a high kick to his face. The man didn't fall, but the impact stunned him. Stiletto moved in close and hammered more blows into a very solid chest, then brought his right hand back, palm up, and sent a death blow into the tip of the man's nose.

The thug's eyes glazed and he fell like a tree, bouncing off the bed before hitting the floor. He lay solidly between Stiletto and the second thug and the woman.

Her wide eyes watched him.

The second thug let her go with a shove, clawing behind his back. Stiletto leaped over the fallen goon and seized the hand holding a pistol. The thug's grip wasn't firm enough, and Scott knocked the gun away.

A hard fist slammed into his midsection and Stiletto doubled over, then a knee smacked into his face. He arced away, losing his footing as he tripped over the first thug. He landed hard on his back.

His hand snaked for the fallen hypodermic as the remaining thug landed on him, striking his face once, twice. The pain was intense, but then Stiletto jabbed the hypo under the thug's right arm.

The needle moved easily through the thug's clothing, meeting momentary resistance as the tip touched flesh. Stiletto pushed it home and hit the plunger with his palm.

The thug screamed and scrambled off Scott, stumbling over his friend. He landed on his back and yanked the needle out of him, his eyes wide and full of fright. The look didn't last long; his body convulsed, his muscles seizing, and he jerked once before lying still.

Stiletto sat up, gasping, his face throbbing. He'd have a few marks to show off at headquarters for sure.

The woman, who had moved to the other side of the bed after being released, made a squeaking noise as she took in the carnage.

"I'm here to help," Stiletto said.

Her voice was hoarse. "Are you a cop?"

"Sort of."

Stiletto stood and leaned against the wall, holding his belly and groaning.

"What does that mean?"

"Federal," he said. "G-Man."

It wasn't a complete lie. It had been the truth at one time. He couldn't very well tell her, "I work for a secret intelligence organization. I'm a spy."

She didn't respond, but she didn't scream either.

"I saw these two following you in the lobby."

"You've been watching me?"

"It was obvious you needed help."

She ran to him, stepping over the body in the way, and examined his face.

"Are you hurt bad?"

"I'll live," Stiletto said. "Been through worse."

"I'm Jennifer."

"Scott."

"Are you a praying man, Scott?"

"A little."

"Well, I've been praying for somebody like you."

"We need to go to my room and talk about this."

"What about these guys?"

He smiled. "We'll let the home office clean up."

The cold water felt good as Stiletto splashed his face. Jennifer Herald sat on the bed, waiting for him. He examined his face in the mirror. The impact marks hadn't revealed themselves yet, but they would by morning. He'd need a good makeup artist to appear normal.

As he wiped his face, Stiletto gave the woman some distance. He remained in the bathroom doorway.

"You've been talking to somebody in the bar," he said. "What's going on?"

She told him.

She was an accountant at Stanton Bridge Group, an architecture firm in Miami owned by a man named Foster

Stanton. The company was making a major push to improve infrastructure in the third world and had selected Chile for one of those projects—a bridge over a wide river the country needed very much. The company was also having financial trouble, and while the blueprints of the bridge specified high-quality steel and components, what had actually made it to the construction site were inferior parts and steel not rated for the load the bridge required, with the company pocketing the difference in cost.

Allegedly, there was proof of the conspiracy in Stanton's office. The plan was to pocket as much money from the project as they could and get the company back in the black, passing off future consequences to the indigenous crew who built the span.

She'd learned about the problem from a since-terminated co-worker she'd dated. *The nervous man*, Scott decided. Charlie, she said, wanted to blow the whistle on the project, but without proof, the media wouldn't listen.

She was staying at the hotel instead of her home because she was afraid of something like today happening. She'd been right. The people at the company knew she and Charlie were talking, and they were willing to go to extremes to stop her.

Scott, being a federal agent, she said, could provide the assistance they needed. Tell Washington or Congress. Tell *somebody* who could open an investigation and stop Stanton.

She stopped. Stiletto made no reply as he considered

her words.

"You say the evidence is in a safe?"

"I'm pretty sure."

"All right."

"What are you going to do?"

"I suppose I can break in and steal it."

"Steal? Don't you, like, need a warrant?"

Stiletto only smiled.

"I need to make some calls," he said.

She looked uncertain. "Okay."

He moved around her to the phone. She left the bed and sat at the writing table against the wall, watching him as he picked up his cell from where it sat beside the hotel phone.

He dialed his boss and waited.

General Isaac Fleming, his chief at Trust headquarters, answered on the third ring.

"You're supposed to be on vacation, Scott."

"You know me, sir," he said. "Trouble is my business."

Fleming's tone turned serious. "What's happening?"

Stiletto took a few minutes to explain. The general remained silent for a moment after Scott finished.

"What would you like to do, Scott?"

"Get the evidence. This sounds like something the Trust should get involved with to me."

"I'm inclined to agree. The potential loss of life and the resulting controversy isn't something we can tolerate. But it's thin, Scott."

"All the more reason for a soft probe to see what's there, sir."

"What do we do with what you find?"

"Leak it to the media. Let them handle the rest. They love a corporate bad guy."

General Ike sighed. "We have operatives in the area who can lend support. What do you need?"

Stiletto gave him a list of various safe-cracking items.

"When might you make your play?"

Stiletto lowered the phone to his chest and asked Jennifer.

"There's a party tomorrow night," she said. "Representatives of the Chilean government will be here to celebrate the start of construction."

He told Fleming about the party.

"Be careful, Scott."

"You know me, sir."

"All too well."

Scott ended the call.

"Guess I'm going to need a suit," he said.

"What about Charlie? If they came for me—"

"Better call and warn him. If you can't reach him, we'll go find him."

She nodded. Scott handed her his phone.

Scott Stiletto did not want to jump out of a perfectly good airplane.

However, security on the street was very tight, and

while Jennifer had an official invitation, it did not include a plus one. It made more sense to break in from the roof rather than approach from the street.

Stiletto gave the pilot of the Cessna, a local Trust agent who had not only provided the plane but the equipment Stiletto had asked headquarters for, a farewell wave and turned to the wide gap to his left where the passenger door had once been. The pilot had removed the door so Stiletto could jump. Scott balked at the two-thousand-foot altitude, and every self-preservation instinct demanded a return to the confines of the airplane cabin. He ignored his mind and pushed away from the Cessna, falling like a rock through the open air.

The night's warm temperature at least made the fall better than had it been forty outside, and as the wind caressed his face and whipped the fabric of his Men's Warehouse suit, he stretched out his arms and legs to slow his fall. He had the roof of the target building in sight. He should land exactly where he wanted.

As gravity pulled him toward the earth, he amused himself by thinking about tonight's adventure. He was breaking into a building to steal something, yes, but not for his own profit. Instead, he was going to steal something that would contribute to the safety of others and expose some real bad guys to the very harsh bright lights of justice.

Stiletto pulled the ripcord and the 'chute billowed from the gray pack on his back, blooming with a violent upward jerk that yanked on the parachute's harness so hard, the straps between Stiletto's legs just about crushed his testicles. He grabbed the risers and steered the 'chute toward the center of the brightly lit roof. The tall building needed the lights so planes wouldn't hit it. The idea seemed perfectly reasonable to Stiletto. The lights made his landing a little easier.

As he drifted ever closer to his destination, Stiletto caught a glimpse of the activity on the street in front of the building. A line of limousines filled the roadway, with more bright lights and the winking flashes of cameras as VIPs arrived for the party.

The party to celebrate the start of construction of a bridge in Chile that would eventually collapse and kill a large number of people.

If Jennifer's information was correct. Stiletto had no reason to believe she was lying. Meeting her had been one of those moments where the God of Justice had pushed Stiletto where He wanted him to go, and Scott had a duty to respond.

The roof zoomed closer, and Stiletto seemed to speed up as he neared. He bent his legs at the knees and felt the hard impact and jolt up his hips, but he didn't fall over as he quickly gathered the 'chute and stripped off the pack. He haphazardly stuffed the material back into the pack and chucked it all in a corner. It wouldn't matter if somebody found it later. There were no markings on the pack or parachute that could lead back to him or the Trust.

Stiletto walked casually toward the door ahead. The door opened on oiled hinges and revealed a staircase that wasn't as brightly lit as the roof. There was enough light for Stiletto to start down the steps while whistling a quiet tune.

It was thirty floors to the lobby where the party was, but he didn't go that far. On the twenty-eighth floor, which was empty of people but contained a farm of cubicles and corner offices, he pressed the call button for an elevator and gratefully stepped into the confines of the car. The descent began.

Stiletto's face took on a grim expression as he mentally prepared to make some very bad men pay for their crimes.

Jennifer Herald's pulse raced. Behaving normally was proving difficult.

The party was in full swing, taking up most of the huge lobby and the ground-floor conference rooms. Music, food, smiles—the festive gathering centered around a large-scale model of a bridge over a river. The bridge in Chile. Not only was the party full of staff, engineers, and company bigwigs, but representatives from the Chilean government were also in attendance. That bothered Jennifer the most. The government representatives had no idea they were staring at a snake in the grass, coiled to strike.

As Jennifer mingled with friends and colleagues and observed Foster Stanton in his tux making jokes with one of the Chilean Interior Ministers, she kept checking her watch. She hoped nobody noticed she was sweating.

She was waiting for the signal.

The fire alarm.

She and Stiletto had no way of communicating with each other. She knew what he was going to do—break into Stanton's office safe—and the only way to signal that he had completed his mission and she should withdraw to their rendezvous was the shrill bleat of the fire alarm.

She drank some champagne from the glass in her left hand, but could barely taste the elixir. Her pulse hammered in her head. How much longer? She wasn't sure she could keep faking her smile.

She had, thankfully, been able to reach Charlie and warn him about her attack. Charlie was hiding out at a new hotel now, waiting for her to bring the evidence from the safe to deliver to the media.

She checked her watch again.

How much longer?

The elevator doors opened on the fifteenth floor.

Foster Stanton, the owner of Stanton Bridge Group, had his office on that floor. It was on the southern side of the building because that side offered the best view of the ocean.

Stiletto stepped onto the thin carpet. He looked left, then right, and saw nobody. The floor was eerily quiet, and if he listened carefully, faint vibrations through the floor signaled the party below was in full swing.

Stiletto removed his dinner jacket and unstrapped the pouch on his back, then put the jacket back on. Carrying the pouch, he started down the walkway between two sets of cubicles toward the double doors at the end. The name-plate on the door simply read STANTON.

An easy lock-pick maneuver popped open the door, which led to a secretary's office, with Stanton's main of-fice across the room. Stiletto ignored the outer office and used the picks on the inner door, opening that with ease and stowing the picks. They would be of no further use to him, and nothing else on this job would be easy.

He approached the painting that hid Stanton's safe. It showed a pack of horses racing through a field of tall grass. Stiletto admired the painting for a moment, taking in the vivid colors and the almost-real eyes of the horse in the lead. It wasn't so much a painting as something real, captured on canvas the way one might capture a photo-graph. As an artist, Stiletto marveled at the technique but had no time to look closer.

The painting swung away from the wall with a gentle pull, and Stiletto examined the stainless-steel door of the safe with the keypad in the center.

It was a medium-sized safe of a make and model Sti-letto had encountered many times before. Four one-inch bolts kept the door in place. He might be able to pry off its hinges from the outside, but the backup hinge on the inside would foil the effort every time, and if it wasn't mounted in the wall, the safe could be dropped from twenty feet and not be damaged.

It had one fatal flaw, however.

He knelt on the floor long enough to open his pouch and took out a heavy magnet and a sock.

The magnet wasn't a garden-variety refrigerator type. It was a neodymium magnet, one of the strongest rare-earth magnets ever invented. He dropped it into the sock.

Rising, he pressed the sock to the door of the safe and let the magnet take hold, then started moving it around. The sock made it easy to move. Stiletto needed to find the nickel solenoid that activated the locking mechanism. Using the magnet meant Stanton would not know his safe had been broken into until he next opened it. Stiletto moved the magnet some more, sharply jerking the handle, and blinked in surprise when the last yank moved the handle into the OPEN position. He pulled on the sock to swing open the door.

As Stiletto slid the powerful magnet off the edge of the door, he glanced at the safe's contents. The two shelves within were quite full, holding envelopes, papers, and jewelry boxes. The yellow manila envelopes caught his eye. There were three. Stiletto dropped the magnet and sock into his right jacket pocket and pulled out all three envelopes, careful not to upset the other contents to the point where they shifted and made closing the door difficult. He did not need to waste time rearranging the items just to make a clean getaway.

He moved to the desk on his right and set the envelopes down. Words in red ink were written on the front side of each, and Stiletto set the one that said CHILE aside. He replaced the other two envelopes in the safe, keeping one of the jewelry boxes from falling out as he did so, and grabbed the handle to close it.

He froze, eyes fixed on the safe's inner doorframe.

"Dammit," he said.

Jennifer Herald might have been able to tell him all about the safe and exactly what to look for, but she apparently didn't know about the magnetic security strip lining the frame. His technique for opening the safe would not have also disengaged the electric connection from the frame to the door, and now an alarm was probably going off somewhere. Security, if they could be pried away from the party, was more than likely on the way up.

Stiletto smiled.

All part of the fun.

He quickly shut the door and moved the picture frame back. The manila envelope went into his pouch, which he then slung across his chest and turned to make his exit. If he could get back to the roof in time—

No dice.

Two security guards in black suits, both on the paunchy side, entered the office. One held a pistol.

"Stop!" the armed guard said.

His partner quickly spoke into a handheld radio, saying that they had one suspect secured and to phone the police.

"What are you doing here?" the armed man said. He held the pistol low, level with his hip, and Stiletto figured if he tried firing from that position, the shot would miss.

"I was just making a sandwich," Stiletto told him.

"You're a long way from the kitchen, buddy."

The guards approached. The unarmed man removed a pair of handcuffs.

"Face the wall."

Stiletto raised his hands and started for the wall, but the guards didn't wait for him to get there like they should have. They met him halfway. As soon as one touched his left arm, Stiletto dropped his right arm, swinging his torso to put some force behind and elbow strike that hammered the armed guard in his soft chest. The man grunted, staggering back. Stiletto pivoted to face the other guard, who still gripped his handheld radio. A snap-kick sent the radio flying from his hand, and a one-two punch to the man's chest and face put him out on the carpet.

The guard with the gun crawled on his hands and knees to where his pistol had fallen and grabbed the gun. Stiletto pulling out the sock with the magnet still at the end and swung, and the hard magnet connected with the steel pistol. The man screaming as a finger cracked too, then Stiletto followed with a kick to the man's face. He rolled over and stopped moving, out cold like his pal.

Stiletto stowed the sock again and straightened his

clothes. He left the office like nothing had happened, and halfway down the hall to the elevator, he pulled the fire alarm. The shrill noise filled the building.

Jennifer Herald followed the crowd of party-goers out of the lobby to the parking lot, the piercing fire alarm un-wavering in its constant blare.

When somebody touched her arm, she snapped her head to the left. Scott Stiletto smiled at her.

"Let's ditch this taco stand," he said.

She was too shocked to answer.

With the police and fire crews arriving, there was enough commotion for the pair to slip away to where Stiletto had parked his getaway car.

"How did they find you?" Jennifer said.

She sat in the passenger seat of Stiletto's Jaguar F-Type as they cruised through traffic, streetlights flashing into the cabin of the car as they passed them.

"You didn't know about the security unit inside the safe."

"Sorry."

"That's okay. I've tripped many alarms in my time."

"Did you—"

"They'll live."

"Good," she said. "What now?"

"Now we go back to my hotel and look over the papers I took," Stiletto said. "And if they prove what your
ex-boyfriend claims, we'll hand them over to the press.
And *then* we get to watch Foster Stanton make a ton of
excuses. Should be fun seeing him squirm."

CHAPTER TWO

General Ike Fleming wasn't used to his new office yet.

At the corner of a busy intersection in Washington, DC, a nondescript single-level gray building stood anonymously. The windows had been blacked out, the exterior paint had faded, and the walls were pock-marked. A perpetual "For Lease" sign hung on one side, but anybody who called the number received a message saying the line had been disconnected.

Nothing about the building stood out unless a passerby wondered why such an eyesore remained standing. Most pedestrians paid it no attention. It was a familiar sight and thus invisible. Anybody breaching the exterior would find only an empty building, the floor covered with debris, and no sign of use.

Beneath the building, it was another story.

Under the street lurked the Washington, DC headquarters of the Trust. The small complex consisted of what the daily crew called the Pit, a cluster of computer workstations with large monitors on the walls. To either side of the Pit were offices and conference rooms. The Pit was where the crew provided support and real-time intelligence for field operatives while also collecting and analyzing incoming information.

The whole setup was new, a replacement after the destruction of the Trust's previous base in the forests of Virginia. Crews were in the process of tearing down the old Virginia base. There would be no going back, and Fleming would miss the quiet of the forest. DC was crowded and noisy, but the new headquarters served the needed purpose.

The Trust wasn't an official apparatus of any nation's intelligence. It was a group run by former intelligence officers who wanted to continue the fight and keep disaster at bay without political interference or red tape.

The new report on Fleming's desk represented such a case.

He turned his chair from the desk and looked at the paintings on the wall. He had no windows to gaze out of, but he had his paintings. They were new because his previous collection had been destroyed in Virginia.

The pictures depicted naval vessels from the eighteenth century, the days of wooden ships and iron men. That was a myth, of course. Those men had faced many of the same difficulties he faced now, hundreds of years later, but he could take no solace from the painting's silence.

General Ike, as he was known around the building, had retired from the Army after a long and decorated career to assume leadership of the CIA's Special Activities Division, a post he'd held for almost as long as he'd worn a uniform. Having been forced out of the Agency by the maneuvers of enemies on Capitol Hill, he now ran the East Coast operations of The Trust.

It was a good place to be. He wasn't ready to hang up his spurs yet.

But this current crisis, the one evidenced by the open file on his desk, gave him one of his migraines. He wanted to be fishing, not wondering how to tell one of his best people that the CIA was planning to assassinate a dear friend for going off the reservation and allegedly murdering a fellow agent.

The intercom on his desk buzzed. The voice of his secretary sounded loud in the quiet room.

"Scott is here, Mr. Fleming."

General Ike grinned. Ms. Griffiths was new to the Trust, but she was an intelligence veteran. Grandmother of two, she tolerated nobody's crap. She knew "General" Ike had never held such a rank; it was a nickname bestowed upon him by colleagues at the CIA. She was the only one in the building who referred to him as "Mister."

He had no intention of correcting her.

He pressed the Talk button. "Send him in, please."

Stiletto, in a suit and tie per the new dress code, drove his car into a parking complex across the street from the anonymous gray building with the blacked-out windows. He parked on the third floor, and via a key, entered an elevator marked PRIVATE. The elevator descended beneath the street and let him off in a cold tunnel. The chill on his neck wasn't from the temperature; the tunnel gave him the creeps. It was the kind of place where any threat could lurk, despite the impossibility of such a prospect.

The light was good, and it enabled him to walk the length of the tunnel to a steel door at the end. He punched a code into a panel and the door unlocked, and he stepped through into the Pit.

Some of the workstation crew looked up and acknowledged his arrival, and he offered a wave in return. If anybody noticed the marks on his face from the fight in Miami, they didn't say anything.

He ignored the images on the screens. The Trust had a constant heavy workload, with operations taking place all over the world. If he took too much time to look at what his colleagues were doing, he'd want to go help. But the general needed him for something else.

Stiletto greeted Ms. Griffiths in her outer office, and she buzzed the boss. He liked her. She was a tough lady with short gray hair, a stern face, and a long career behind her. She'd joined the Trust to settle down in one place after years of global postings.

When he entered Fleming's office, he found the general behind the desk.

"Enjoy your time off?" Fleming said.

Stiletto smiled. "Sure. Still not used to this place, though."

Fleming laughed. "We look like a pair of corporate attorneys, if you were an attorney who insisted on getting into bar fights."

"You always did. I'm used to street clothes. This dress code is for the birds. How do you tolerate a tie every day?"

"The secret is a clip-on," Fleming disclosed.

Stiletto took the seat in front of the general's desk. "I never would have guessed."

"Spymasters are experts at manipulation." Fleming sat down too. His smile vanished.

"Is it bad?" Stiletto said.

"We'll get to that in a minute. First, I need to talk to you about jumping out of an airplane over Miami."

Stiletto smiled.

"Are you happy with the effort?"

"That Stanton fellow was putting lives at risk to line his pockets. You know me, General. I can't let go of something like that."

"From what I'm seeing, I don't disagree. The news today is that other whistleblowers are coming forward to back up the statements of the two people you worked with."

"Good."

"You should stick your nose where it doesn't belong more often."

"Don't tempt me, sir."

He and Fleming shared a quiet laugh, but Scott didn't like the chit-chat. It wasn't like the general. He was nervous about why the man needed Scott's help.

Stiletto waited.

"Now, as to the other thing," Fleming finally said. "When was the last time you spoke with John Pike?"

Stiletto blinked. He hadn't been expecting the question.

"Boy," he said, "how many years ago did I join CIA?"

"He recruited you, correct?"

"After my wife passed, yeah. And after my daughter quit talking to me."

Fleming knew the subject of Stiletto's family was a painful one, but Scott was not averse to talking about it, probably because he hoped to figure out why his daughter had cut him out of her life. She never answered his calls, although he phoned dutifully on Christmas and her birthday, always hoping for an answer. She had ignored every call so far.

"It's not good news."

"What's happened?"

"Two weeks ago, he vanished. He left the office and dropped out of sight. Two days ago, a CIA agent on vacation in San Francisco spotted him on the street, talking to an as-yet-unidentified woman. That agent, William Strong, was later found dead in an alley. Shot twice."

CHAPTER THREE

Stiletto didn't believe it.

John Pike was the man who'd pulled Scott out of his depressive state after the double-whammy death of his wife and estrangement of his daughter.

It had been Pike who'd offered Stiletto a chance to get his life back together by suggesting he start a career with the Central Intelligence Agency. He'd helped guide Scott through six months of grueling interviews, until finally, Stiletto had been accepted to the CIA's training academy and began working for General Ike in the Special Activities Division.

They'd been in and out of touch over the last few years since both had been busy with various assignments. Stiletto's dismissal from the CIA had caused a larger distance to grow between them, but he maintained warm thoughts and affection for the pal who had come through when he'd really needed a friend.

Stiletto said, "What is the CIA saying about Johnny?"

"Strong reported making contact with Pike and scheduling a meet. Strong showed up to the meet and wound up dead."

"They think John shot him?"

"Yes."

"It can't be true, sir. You know him as well as I do."

"That's right, I do. I don't believe it either. But he has a lot of questions to answer, and he's not making himself available to answer them."

"There has to be a reason."

"I'm sure there is."

"Is that why we're having this conversation?"

General Ike nodded. "I still have some friends at the CIA. I've asked for a few days to look into this. If we can't come up with any answers, the kill teams are going out. John Pike will have a target on his back, shoot on sight."

Stiletto's face was grim, his lips pressed together and his jaw tight.

"You have your FBI contact in San Francisco, right?"

"Toby O'Brien, yeah."

"The Bureau has taken over the investigation, and they're keeping Strong's Agency affiliation quiet. We need to know if he left anything behind that can help."

"How much time?" Scott said.

"A week, maybe less. Depends on how things develop,

and I can't say the CIA won't take the case back from us should we prove Strong was killed by somebody other than Pike. Regardless, after a week, the dogs go out."

Stiletto rose from the chair and smoothed the front of his suit. "We'd better not waste any more time talking."

"See Ms. Griffiths on your way out. She has a plane ticket for San Francisco."

Stiletto nodded.

"Good luck, Scott."

"This one's personal, sir." Stiletto started for the door. "You can bet I won't overlook anything."

"It's always personal for you."

Stiletto paused with his hand on the doorknob and looked back at the boss. Yeah, jobs *were* always personal to Scott. It was easier to fight for people than ideals. People made ideals possible. Stiletto saw himself as somebody who could speak for the defenseless. His adventure in Miami had simply been another example of that philosophy in action.

And now, one of his closest friends was in danger of being killed by the very government he'd sworn to serve.

"You're right, sir. Nothing ever changes."

Stiletto left the office.

Harrison Joule stood at the top of a hill and smiled as he reflected that his career had begun at this anonymous spot in Northern Ireland. It showed no sign of slowing down.

He was older now, of course, and more interested in having the young bucks go into the field to do the dirty work while he arranged the chessboard behind the scenes. His latest scheme would endear him to the young freedom fighters of the world like nothing else.

As long as he cleared the obstructions first.

There was always one. Always somebody in the group who would betray the others for his or her own gain.

Behind Joule stood a two-bedroom log cabin with a thatched roof and a small garden, with an unfettered view of the Irish countryside. Rolling green hills stretched for miles no matter where he looked, made more magnificent by the clear blue sky and crisp morning temperature. Joule was bundled in a heavy coat and holding a steaming mug of tea. And he wasn't drinking English Breakfast, either. He still had Irish Nationalist sympathies and despised the Northern occupation. He realized, though, that the British were probably there to stay.

He took a long drink of the hot liquid as two Land Rovers rounded the bend at the far end of the dirt road leading to the cabin. They moved at a moderate pace, not kicking up any dust or debris, traveling casually along the rough track to the cabin. Joule checked his watch. They were on time, but he expected nothing less.

The door of the cabin opened behind him.

"All set in here," the man in the doorway said. He was big, and he didn't come out because he'd have to bend over to avoid bumping his head. He had a barrel chest, and his name was Lagros. He was Joule's hatchet man. If Joule pointed at somebody, Lagros went for the kill. His big hands never failed to leave behind a corpse.

"Very good, Lagros," Joule said. "Hang out in the back while we have our discussion. I'll need you afterward."

"Okay."

The big man stepped back and shut the door.

Presently, the Land Rovers came to a stop in front of the cabin. Three men exited each Rover, the drivers remaining inside. The men carried nothing. Cell phones were not allowed at the cabin. Joule had a sophisticated electronic detection system wired into the front doorway. If anybody came in with a cell phone or any kind of recording or transmitting device, an alarm would sound. Joule would then deal with that person most lethally.

Astute members of the public would never recognize the faces of his guests, but members of the international intelligence community and law enforcement might take note of two or three of the men who had obvious criminal connections. Joule had pulled them from the underworld haunts he had inhabited for decades.

Harrison Joule had begun as a bomb maker for the IRA and graduated to various mercenary endeavors, including several stints in Africa in the '80s and '90s. He'd carried out bomb attacks for a number of Middle Eastern jihad groups in Europe, including a particularly bloody campaign in Paris, before finally realizing that the men who provided the arms and material to the fighters made more money and didn't have to evade bullets. Then he began providing weapons and explosives and personnel when the price was right.

As the number of candles on the birthday cake increased, he was glad for the decision. He was still relatively unknown to Western Intelligence, thanks to his use of cutouts and blinds that kept his identity concealed.

For their current project, Joule and his men were working on spec. No client, but they expected a bidding war for the product they would soon offer.

Joule greeted the men one by one and showed them into the cabin. The meeting was about to begin.

CHAPTER FOUR

The interior of the cabin was equally rustic and spartan—wood floor with plenty of throw rugs. No electricity, so the only light came through the windows. Raw logs made up the walls and ceiling. It wasn't a cabin for a long-term stay. It was a cabin for short visits and secret meetings.

Joule was pleased his doorway sensor hadn't detected any electronic devices. He ushered the group to the table in the center of the room, where several pitchers of water and appropriate glasses were laid out, and everybody took a seat. Joule sat at the head of the table.

"Thank you all for being here."

Joule scanned the eager faces. The Americans were James Fox and Oscar DeSoto. The latter was a big man in a room full of slender ones. The Eastern Europe representatives were Vracek and Pavic. The Brits, Gambelin and Tunison.

Joule continued, "I won't bore you with a silly preamble. We know what we're here for. We are going to assemble a pair of missiles tipped with chemical warheads and auction the missiles to the highest bidder."

The group made noises of agreement.

Joule said, "Mr. Pavic, the latest, please?"

Pavic was younger than Joule, with a bony chin and hair that looked dry. He didn't need to consult any notes. That was another rule with Joule. *Write nothing down.*

"Morgan Lane," Pavic said, "has agreed to our price, and she will deliver two canisters of a chemical agent that we can place inside the missiles."

"Who did she buy from?"

"A former ISIS member named Mahfi," Pavic said. "They had some trouble in Berlin. The Russians, they think. Mahfi is dead, but she has the weapon."

Joule said, "Excellent. The Russians saved us a bullet. Our man Marco Diego is in charge of field operations and collecting the components to build the missiles. He is on schedule. Oscar? The tubes?"

"Construction is complete," Oscar DeSoto said.

Joule nodded. "Then the missiles will be completed in the next few days. The auction invitations, by the way, have gone out. We are expecting a high turnout."

He didn't need to explain to the crew that the invitations were word of mouth only. Joule wasn't going to violate his security protocols.

"That's all for today," Joule announced. "Dismissed."

Joule remained seated as the other men rose to leave. He asked Fox and Vracek to remain. Fox and Vracek looked nervous. Fox wiped the sweat from his forehead, and Joule noticed the subtle movement. It was too early and too chilly for anybody to sweat.

Joule folded his hands on his lap. Fox and Vracek sat next to each other on the left side of the table as Joule faced it. Joule said, "Stand up, Mr. Vracek."

The man with the wire-framed glasses, his face calm, stood. Joule called, "Mr. Lagros!"

A door behind Joule opened, and the big man ducked to enter the room. Fox watched the new arrival with wide eyes.

"Mr. Vracek, you forgot that I still have friends in the IRA, and when you went to them to try and sell me out, they told me everything."

Vracek said quickly, "But I didn't!" His normally pale face blanched further. He opened his mouth to argue some more, but by then, Lagros was on him. The barrel-chested man used his big hands to snap Vracek's neck. He grunted with the effort, but it didn't take more than one try. Vracek's body quickly went limp and collapsed to the floor.

"Put him out back," Joule said. "Then I have more for you to do."

The big man hoisted Vracek over his shoulder and carried him outside.

Fox let out a breath.

"Made you nervous?" Joule grinned. Fox worked out of Greece and was in charge of shipping operations. He had worked with Joule on several African adventures and was quite trustworthy. Joule knew he'd never have a reason to have Lagros break his neck.

The American nodded. "Yes."

"You have nothing to worry about."

"I know that, but still. Lagros can make anybody nervous. What happened?"

"My IRA pals told me some of the new kids took Vracek up on the information, and now they're trying to interfere with our project. We have to warn our people."

"Do they want the missiles for themselves?"

"Only the detonators," Joule said. "They aren't interested in the chemical agent."

"Won't the IRA stop them?"

Joule shook his head. "The old-timers I worked with have no influence on the new leadership. They won't kill their own. We will have to take care of the issue ourselves."

"I'll get the message to Diego."

"How's the new man?" Joule said.

"Very good," Fox replied. "His charms have had an effect on Elsa, I hear."

"He's old enough to be her father."

Fox looked up and grinned. "So are you."

"But my charms *didn't* work on her. Pardon me if I'm jealous. I'm going to have to meet him eventually. I'd like to see what it took to sway Elsa because whatever it is, I'm not fortunate enough to have it."

Lagros returned to the cabin. He ducked under the doorway, shut the door, and approached the table as Joule gestured to an empty chair. The big man sat to Joule's right.

"Vracek passed information to some IRA shooters in Belfast, and they are going to try and intercept the detonators," he told Lagros. "I want you to stop them."

Lagros nodded.

Fox said, "It can never be easy, can it?"

Joule shook his head.

CHAPTER FIVE

Stiletto passed through security at Reagan National Airport and realized he was starving.

He ordered at a small burger place and decided he would be no help to Johnny if he didn't take care of himself. He had to stay focused, which meant staying hydrated and fed. Like always. This mission was nothing new. There had been many friends in danger, most recently General Ike and his wife, Betsie, but this time, because it was Johnny Pike, Stiletto was ignoring the basics and racing to his destination to solve the problem.

Stiletto occupied a booth in a back corner, facing the door. Music from wall-mounted speakers drowned out the other patrons' voices. The hardwood booth was not comfortable in the least. He figured people weren't meant to stay long, so perhaps there was a method to the madness of the design.

He washed down the meal with a glass of ice water. With two hours still to kill before his flight, he next wandered to a bar and nursed a Makers-and-Coke while watching people come and go. Most of the travelers were tired businesspeople who had the same faraway stare on their faces as he did, but for a different reason.

A cleaning crew ran a polishing machine over the walkway tiles, the grind of the motor sounding vaguely like a washing machine. They didn't hold his interest, so he stared into the drink. The Makers-and-Coke shimmered a little as the overhead light reflected in the glass.

He and Pike had served together in the same Special Forces unit and quickly forged a bond. They had similar interests in cars and music, and for somebody like Scott, who had been dragged around the world by his career Army father—and as a result, had trouble making friends well into adulthood—Pike's fellowship was most welcome. They'd shared triumph and tragedy. Pike had lost his wife and child, too.

Pike and his pregnant wife had been in Paris, enjoying a vacation, when a car bomb exploded outside a post office. Pike's pregnant wife had died in the blast. Pike, wounded, was rushed back to the United States, and Stiletto and the other Green Berets on their team had helped get him through the next few years. It had taken a lot to put John Pike back together, and he still missing a few pieces that could never be replaced.

Stiletto finished his drink and ordered another.

When Scott's wife died, Pike had shown up. They'd never specifically addressed what happened. Pike had come simply to be there, and his presence meant a lot to Scott. It had meant even more after his daughter, Felicia, took off. It wasn't quite the same, but even Pike had admitted Stiletto might be feeling like he had truly lost both.

Every now and then, Pike had dug through the files, looking for information on who might have set off the bomb in Paris. He was looking for answers, for clues, for somebody to go after. As far as Stiletto knew, he had never found what he was looking for.

And then the proverbial lightbulb flashed over his head.

Did Johnny's sudden disappearance and the situation in San Francisco have to do with his family's murder?

Stiletto finished his second drink and decided against a third. He went to the departure gate. When the plane finally boarded, he dropped into his seat and strapped in.

San Francisco. It wasn't his first visit. The last time he'd been there, an old girlfriend named Ali Lewis had needed help discovering who'd murdered her father. He had left with a question between them. Could Stiletto leave his globe-trotting behind and settle down? Perhaps use his drawing skills (he was a self-taught artist) to contribute to her fashion company's designs? They had elected not to answer then, and he wasn't going back to see her now. He had other matters to attend to, and short of bumping into her on the street, he had no plans to look her up. She surely had moved on with her life by now, and Stiletto was nowhere on her radar. It was best not to re-open that wound.

It would be nice to see Toby O'Brien again, though. He'd had helped with the Lewis mission, and had also assisted Scott on another assignment across the bay in Berkeley.

A long time ago.

Stiletto dozed off.

After landing at San Francisco International Airport, Stiletto hopped into a cab and told the driver to take him to the Embarcadero Hyatt. The driver raced up 101 North into downtown SF, where street noise combined with traffic to produce a crushing sensation Stiletto hadn't experienced before. Constructions crews were everywhere, tearing up the street.

He checked in at the Hyatt, and once in his room, he undressed, showered, and then sat on the edge of the bed. He left the drapes closed. It was an old habit he didn't think he was ever going to break. The details of the room were lost on him. He was focused on what sat directly within reach, the white plastic telephone with stickers listing which phone numbers to call for room service or emergency.

He picked up the handset and dialed. He knew O'Brien's number by heart. No need for a sticker to remind him.

CHAPTER SIX

"Don't tell me," O'Brien said after Stiletto had said hello. "Let me guess."

Stiletto did not reply. He smiled. It was good to hear Toby's voice.

"This is Publishers Clearinghouse, finally calling to tell me I've won enough money to tell the Bureau to stick it."

"Nope," Scott said.

"Well, hearing from the great Scott Stiletto isn't terrible. Where have you been?"

Stiletto started to answer, but the words didn't come out. Where did he start?

"I've been all over the world and back again," he said instead. The rest of the story could wait until later.

"The number you're calling from is here in the city."

"Yeah, I'm at the Hyatt."

"Business or pleasure?"

"Business, I'm afraid. Can you talk for a bit?"

"Sure, what's happening?"

Stiletto and O'Brien had met in the Army during Basic Training. They were taking different MOS specialties but had ultimately reconnected at the JFK Special Warfare Center, where O'Brien worked logistics while Stiletto deployed with an A-Team. O'Brien knew John Pike, too. Scott was breaking the rules to bring the FBI man in on the mission, but he didn't care. He could trust O'Brien, and Toby deserved to know what was happening. The more he knew, the more he could help. And Stiletto had to admit he knew very little to begin with.

He certainly wasn't going to discuss matters on an open line, so they made dinner plans. O'Brien showed up after seven, and they ate in the hotel's steakhouse. Halfway through the story, O'Brien was already making calls to check on the case. He knew they had taken over something from SFPD, but he wasn't clear on all the details.

Presently, O'Brien ended his series of calls.

"Body's still at the morgue. We can check him out in the morning."

"Any idea what to do with the rest of the night?"

O'Brien offered only a half-grin in return, his eyes a little sad.

"It's okay, Toby. I know you have a family."

"Old lady's expecting me before nine."

Stiletto didn't understand why O'Brien felt the need to tiptoe around the fact that his wife and two kids were doing very well indeed, but the FBI man always shied away from the subject. Had they seen each other more often,

Stiletto might have been more annoyed by the behavior.

"I'll find something to do around here."

"Don't get into any trouble. I'll pick you up at seven in the morning. Make sure you shower and shave. The morgue is a classy place."

Stiletto tried to stop himself, but upon returning to the hotel room, he felt restless, so he grabbed his cell phone and dialed Ali Lewis's number. But he didn't press Send. Why did he want to talk to her after earlier deciding not to? But it was almost nine o'clock, and the urge to hear her voice spoke louder than good sense. Maybe she'd be home. He pressed Send.

The line rang once, and she answered.

"Scott?"

Stiletto jumped at the sound of her voice. There might always be some residual feelings for Ali Lewis, former CIA colleague and now the owner of an international fashion company, but did he really still have feelings, or did he only see her as a lifeline to get away from his current situation?

Because there were times when he wanted out very badly.

But not most of the time.

"Is something wrong?" she said when he didn't reply.

"Hi, Ali," he said. "No, nothing is wrong. I'm in San Francisco again."

"Can you talk about it?"

"Not really."

She laughed. "Same old story. How have you been?"

"I have no idea where to start on that one. I'm not with the Company anymore."

"What happened?"

Stiletto chuckled humorlessly. Again, where could he start? "I did something that got me fired, then tried freelancing for a while, but that didn't work out."

"Are you looking for work?"

"No, I have a job."

"Okay, well, I have a date tonight, so I'm in the middle of getting ready. If you're in town for long, we can probably get a drink."

Stiletto said nothing.

"Scott?"

"I'm here. I wasn't expecting you to say that."

This time, Ali paused. He didn't ask if she was still on the line.

"Scott, we never made any promises to each other. I mean, it's just dinner. I don't think—"

"Ali, you don't owe me an explanation. I wanted to see how you were doing, that's all."

"Okay. It's good to hear your voice."

"Yours too."

"I gotta go, Scott."

"Have fun tonight."

He let her hang up first and spent the rest of the night

alone in the quiet room.

The next morning, after sitting in traffic for forty-five minutes, Toby O'Brien parked his government car at the San Francisco Medical Examiner's office, and he and Scott entered the dull gray building.

Stiletto didn't talk much during the drive, his mind filled with thoughts of both Pike and Ali Lewis. Toby must have sensed something was bothering him because he didn't try to get a conversation going during the drive.

In the basement where they kept the coolers, Scott and Toby pushed open a pair of swinging doors, which showed a myriad of scuffs and dents from being banged open by too many gurneys. The chill hit Stiletto right away like a smack in the face, but it didn't faze O'Brien.

The cooler drawers lined the walls. Steel tables, some unoccupied, others covered with sheets, were spaced out on the open floor. The junior medical examiner in attendance consulted a wall chart that identified which cooler contained which body and directed O'Brien and Stiletto to Cooler 4004.

O'Brien pulled the drawer open with a grunt. It slid out on tracks, the wheels squealing, a cloud of frost hanging in the air for a moment. And there was William Strong, his body bag half-open, looking as if he were asleep.

Stiletto tilted his head and examined the dead man's face. He hadn't known him. He had no idea if he and Strong had anything in common, or if they'd have been polar opposites. All he knew was that Strong was in a box, dead and cold, while Stiletto was looking for a reason. He did feel bad that Strong's family would be told he had died as a random crime victim. No way would the CIA reveal the truth. The incident was ready-made for a cover-up. That was the spy business.

Stiletto knew for sure that somebody had murdered William Strong, but he didn't think Johnny Pike was guilty. Whoever had pulled the trigger deserved the kind of retribution only Stiletto could deliver. He owed William Strong that much, even if they'd never met. Someday it might be him in the cooler, and he hoped the investigating agent shared the same concern.

The dead man had been well-built. His hair was shaggy, and he had a variety of scars on his upper body. William Strong had seen some action, for sure.

Toby O'Brien said, "Is this him?"

Stiletto shrugged. "I guess. Any details on what happened at the crime scene?"

"Cops canvassed the area where the shooting happened, and then my people went through a second time, but we didn't get any clear picture of the suspect."

"No witnesses?"

"Time of death was close to three in the morning," O'Brien said. "The only people hanging around were the derelicts living on the street, and most of them were either drunk or drugged into oblivion."

"Any personal effects?"

"Locked up until the body is claimed."

"Where was he staying?"

"The Marriott on 4th and Mission. Room's still sealed."

"Can we go there?"

"Sure."

At the busy Marriott Hotel, they found William Strong's room at the end of the tenth-floor hallway. The crime scene tape across the door had not been disturbed. O'Brien slit the tape with a pocketknife and used a key card to pop the lock. He pushed open the door.

Stiletto entered behind him.

With the victim in the morgue, the visit felt unusual. Stiletto was about to rifle through William Strong's stuff. It had to be done, but it gave the same strange feeling he'd had in the morgue.

"I suppose you know what you're looking for," O'Brien said.

"Not really."

The first thing Stiletto's eyes landed on was the laptop on the desk, but he didn't go for it straight away. He pawed through the nightstand, the clothes in the dresser drawers, and the suitcases in the closet. Strong had come to San Francisco on vacation, and by all appearances, had planned to make the most of the visit.

Stiletto finally went to the laptop. He unplugged the cord and wrapped it, holding the lightweight machine under one arm. "I think this is all I need."

O'Brien held the door, and they left the room.

CHAPTER SEVEN

Stiletto placed the computer on the table in his hotel room and stared at the machine, letting out a breath. He needed there to be something of value to be on the hard drive. Having Strong's cell phone might have been nice, but asking O'Brien to dig it out of evidence was probably too much to ask.

The computer posed its own issues. He might need a professional hacking job to unlock the machine, which meant calling headquarters, but then he remembered it wasn't an official CIA computer. It was William Strong's personal laptop. He might not have anything difficult to overcome.

He eased back in the chair and turned to look around the dark room. The only light came from the crack in the still-closed drapes. He went to the wall and flipped switches until the lights were all on, and for the first time, really saw his room.

He removed his shoes and socks and enjoyed the feel

of the soft carpet, then opened the drapes, lifted the window, and let in the salt-scented air. The hotel was right on the edge of the bay's waters, and there was no longer a reason for him to keep the drapes closed. He might as well find a way to enjoy himself, even if he remained confined to the room.

From room service, he ordered a burger with fries and a large Coke. After eating, he finally turned his attention back to the laptop. He lifted the lid and pressed the power button, and the computer booted to the password prompt. Stiletto stared at the white box. He'd need to hack the computer after all.

He called General Ike and talked to him over his cell phone speaker.

"I need to get into this computer, General. It's a personal unit, not CIA issue."

"Hang on."

General Ike put him on hold. Stiletto picked at the leftover French fries. They were the large wedge-shaped fries that filled one's belly faster than thin-cut fries, and Stiletto could never eat them without feeling like he'd had a potato overdose.

"Scott?"

"Here, sir."

"I have Gordon Duncan from our technical section here."

"Hi, Gordon."

"I need a pathway to get into this machine," the technical wizard said. "Can you plug your phone in with the charging unit and turn on the wi-fi?"

Stiletto complied without asking any questions. Instead, he answered Duncan's questions about the IP address of the hotspot created by his phone, and then Duncan found a way into the machine through an "open socket" that Stiletto barely understood. He watched as Duncan took over the computer, the cursor flashing across the screen as he manipulated the unit, clicking deeper into the laptop's system files and hacking the password prompt. The process gained access to the desktop in less than five minutes.

"Is that all?" Duncan asked. He sounded like he hacked ten laptops before breakfast. This was easy work for him.

"For now, yes," Scott replied. "General, are you staying on while I look through this?"

"Might as well."

Stiletto went to work. He started clicking through William Strong's personal files, and in the My Pictures folder, he found a file marked SF.

He clicked on it.

Digital pictures filled the screen.

"He took a lot of touristy photos," Stiletto said, scrolling through the images. "Probably all transferred from his phone, which makes not having that less of an issue."

"Uh-huh," General Ike said.

Stiletto clicked one picture and activated the slide show option, scrolling through each picture as it filled the screen. It wasn't until she neared the end that he found a shot that froze him in place.

"Are you there, Scott?"

"I have something."

"Tell me."

"Two shots of Johnny. There's a blonde woman with him. She's wearing a white pantsuit in both and carrying a diamond-studded mini-purse. There's a third shot at a sidewalk restaurant. Strong aimed the camera under a table, but I think this is where he messed up. The woman is looking right at him."

"Upload those pictures. We'll get an ID on her."

Stiletto closed the slide show, put the photos in a separate folder, and emailed the pics to Fleming.

"On the way."

"Anything else?"

Stiletto closed the folder and examined the desktop. A text file named Log jumped out at him. He clicked it.

"I found a log," he said. "Strong only made a few notes. Initial sighting of Pike, contact with his CIA boss, all that."

"Where was the first sighting?"

"Cupid's Arrow."

"Which is where? And *what?*"

"Down the street near the water," Stiletto said. "It's a huge bow on the Embarcadero, embedded into the cement. Local landmark. I'll check it out and call you back."

Stiletto ended the call and grabbed his shoes.

CHAPTER EIGHT

Lagros, Harrison Joule's assassin, had just arrived in Belfast to find the crew linked with the man who'd betrayed the group. He reached his hotel room and activated the deadbolt and the swing bolt. He'd been given a large suite with a deck at a Holiday Inn near the George Best airport. He went to the heater/AC unit near the deck doors and turned up the heat, and with a low hum, a blast of warm air filled the room.

He placed his suitcase on the bed and removed the X-ray-proof bottom. From the hidden compartment, he took out his customized Wilson Combat .45 automatic, a box of subsonic ammo, and a framed photograph.

The gun, ammo, and silencer, he stored in the nightstand drawer. The picture he set with care on the nightstand next to the lamp. He looked at the ponytailed girl in the frame: dark hair, big smile, blue eyes. Lagros took a cigar and a lighter from his inside jacket pocket, opened the patio door, and stepped outside. He lit up, stared out into the night, and thought of his daughter. He'd never see her again face to face, and it was better that way. Police in three countries wanted him for various murders, and he didn't want them or any enemies looking for revenge using her as leverage. He'd made his choices long ago and was at peace with suffering for them. His daughter didn't deserve punishment for his sins. He hoped her mother had found another man to take his place and help raise her right.

Lagros smoked his cigar and enjoyed the coolness of the evening before showering and climbing into bed.

Harrison Joule had contracted with a small-time arms dealer named Ferguson for the needed detonators, the very items at risk that Lagros had to keep out of IRA hands.

Lagros found the small-statured Irishman at a pub, where he ate alone in a corner booth in the back. The eyes of other patrons followed Lagros as he entered. They knew he was from out of town. He didn't fit in at all. He was bigger than most, and his obvious Greek features stood out.

The assassin ignored them and slid into the booth opposite Ferguson, who froze with a sandwich halfway to his mouth.

"Keep eating," Lagros said, his voice low. "Joule sent me."

Ferguson swallowed his bite and said, "The Vracek situation. I'm aware."

"You know where the IRA team is?"

"I can put you on the trail, yeah."

"How many?"

"Four. Led by a man named Kevin O'Rourke."

Lagros nodded.

"They've been following me off and on," Ferguson said, "but I'm of no use to them currently."

"Why?"

"The detonators aren't here. I sent them ahead for when I meet with your people."

"But they can follow you to where you're going."

"Certainly."

"How do I find them?"

"O'Rourke has a girlfriend. I know where she lives. Her name is Sally Brogan."

Ferguson put down his sandwich and took a pen from the pocket of his shirt. He scribbled on a napkin and passed it to Lagros, who folded it into his coat.

"You need to get out of town," the big man said.

"I will, don't worry."

Lagros slid out of the booth. The eyes followed him to the door.

Doing nothing wasn't in Sally Brogan's nature, but orders were orders.

O'Rourke had made it clear that the cell could do no more until they secured the needed detonators, and conflicts with the Provos as well as the usual interference from Special Branch and MI5 necessitated keeping a low profile for the time being.

She did normal things like shopping and strolling and reading in the park. She didn't have an office to go to; the Real IRA was her occupation, her life, and her family's legacy.

Sally Brogan had been born to a family deeply involved in the Irish struggle against the British, as far back as the Easter Rising of '17 and well into the Troubles. Her older brother, Billy, had been shot and killed in a gun battle with the Royal Ulster Constabulary, and she, on the run at the time and hiding in Spain, had been unable to attend his funeral. She harbored a hatred for the Brits like no other.

She was part of the "Real" IRA that had formed in 1997, splitting from the Provisional IRA because its members did not accept the ceasefire organized between the Brits and IRA to end hostilities in Northern Ireland and commit to a peace process that would leave the North split from the rest of Ireland. That was not in any way an achievement of the goals stated by the IRA. Too many had died for people like Sally to accept what was essentially a surrender of their ideals and an acceptance of British control.

MI5 had put intense pressure on the Real IRA cells in recent months, along with further pressure from the Provisional IRA, who had never accepted the RIRA's status as part of the rebellion. While MI5 focused on arresting known RIRA players, the Provos sabotaged their weapons dumps, making it nearly impossible for RIRA cells to carry on with their current bombing campaign.

Her boyfriend had developed a plan to strike back, but the RIRA council had vetoed the idea. They were going to carry out the plan anyway, but they needed Ferguson's detonators to make their bombs work.

It would have been preferable to kill Ferguson and steal the parts, but that wasn't a possibility. Ferguson knew them well and knew how to cover his bases. Their chance to buy or steal the detonators would come when Ferguson met with Joule's people, but they didn't know his timetable, so they had the arms dealer under surveillance.

Sally had met Kevin O'Rourke in 2009 when the two of them and one other operative had successfully smuggled two crates of automatic rifles from Croatia into Northern Ireland. Since that time, they'd been inseparable. O'Rourke had changed addresses often, while Sally had been able to hold down an apartment. The lease was not in her right name, which provided a small amount of protection.

She ate lunch at a park, watching people come and go, and finally returned to her apartment a little after one o'clock. She performed her usual countersurveillance routine, and by the time she unlocked the door, she knew she was clear of any watchers who might have been covering her trail.

Sally placed her purse, cell phone, and apartment keys

on the kitchen counter.

Then somebody knocked on the door.

Sally didn't answer.

She was naturally paranoid about unscheduled contacts and home visits. If anybody needed to reach her, they called first. The person at the door could be an innocent person or a Special Branch agent.

Her visitor wrapped knuckles on the door again three times.

A peek through the spy hole showed a barrel-chested man in black. She didn't recognize him. He was alone, or at least, there was nobody else in view. It didn't mean anything. He could have a squad of armed men on either side of the door. She collected a nine-millimeter Glock from the pocket of a long coat hanging beside the door.

She stepped back, her finger off the trigger of the Glock. Hopefully, the man would go away.

Instead, the man spoke, his deep voice coming loud and clear through the door.

"I know you're in there, Sally."

A chill raced up her spine. She retreated to the kitchen for her cell phone and put the gun down on the counter long enough to start a text to Kevin. And then the door smashed open with a solid kick from the other side.

She was dressed for running, as always, in jeans, a t-shirt, and tennis shoes. But the big man moved fast, closing the gap between her and the door, a gun in his right fist. She grabbed for the Glock, but it was too late.

The big man kicked her in the stomach.

Breath left her in a rush, and pain exploded through her body. She collapsed, remembering to keep her grip on the gun. Her mouth was wide open, but she couldn't breathe.

"Where's O'Rourke?" the man said.

He lifted his gun at the same time she raised the Glock. She put pressure on the trigger as the big man's gun thumped twice, the shots muffled by the snout of a suppressor. The gun fell from her fingers as fiery pain filled her body, different from the pain related to being kicked. A spray of tissue and blood spread across the kitchen floor beneath her, then her vision faded. The last thing she saw was the man frowning at her.

Lagros lowered his gun with a sigh.

The woman was no good to him dead, and there was no sense in trying to put her back together. He hadn't fired to wound her.

He kicked the Glock across the floor, and it bumped against a wall. Picking up the cell phone, he examined the screen. Her incomplete text to O'Rourke was still there, and he found the IRA man's phone number on her contact list. He went back to the text box and finished her message.

Somebody is at my door!

Lagros dropped the phone in a pocket and exited the apartment.

He wouldn't have to go looking for O'Rourke. When Sally failed to answer her phone, he'd come looking for her.

"Why isn't she answering her phone?"

Kevin O'Rourke wanted to reach through the cell phone and strangle Sean Collins. Normally, Sean could be counted on to know what O'Rourke was thinking before he voiced what was on his mind. Today, not so much, and O'Rourke's stress level was high enough that he wasn't in the mood for brain farts.

"I'm sorry, Kevin. That was a stupid question."

O'Rourke calmed himself with a deep breath as he steered through traffic.

"It was no accident," O'Rourke said, "that we heard about Vracek. Joule may be sending a clean-up squad."

"Kevin—"

"Or what? Tip off MI5? Not Joule's style. Tell the others. We need to grow eyes in the backs of our heads."

"Call me when you get to her," Collins said.

"Right."

O'Rourke ended the call and tossed the cell phone on the passenger seat. A curse escaped his lips as he stopped for a red light.

Kevin O'Rourke did not look like a starved terrorist on the run. He was a burly fellow with a thick mustache and more around the middle than he wanted to admit. But he was in charge of a cell, which had been a goal of his since joining the IRA in his early twenties.

He became another "pioneer" member of the Real IRA when the split with the Provos happened in 1997. The Army Council had taken a liking to him straight away, putting him in charge of his four-person cell, with orders to conduct operations independently from the main hive but to stay in close contact for when larger operations required more bodies.

He rose in the ranks and received the promotion to team leader after the Massereene Barracks shooting in 2009, where two British soldiers were killed, two others wounded, and two pizza delivery men hurt as well. O'Rourke hadn't been one of the shooters, but he'd organized the getaway, spiriting the gunmen out of Northern Ireland to a safe haven in Spain.

He alternated wiping his sweaty palms on his trousers as he made the turn into the parking garage of Sally's complex.

The low light and gray concrete floor, walls, and support columns put him instantly on alert. O'Rourke steered into a handicapped spot and left the car and at a crooked angle as he exited, sliding a hand under his coat for a Browning Hi-Power semi-automatic pistol.

He stopped short as his cell rang.

"Sally?"

"Turn around."

O'Rourke knew better. The male voice echoed behind

him. He dived beside his car, landing painfully on the hard concrete as two suppressed rounds split the air where he'd been. One smacked into a taillight of his car. O'Rourke stayed flat while turning himself around, then scrambled closer to the rear passenger-side tire and leaned around the back with the Browning tight in his fist. The shooter wore black and was approaching at a steady pace from the other side of the garage. O'Rourke didn't need somebody to tell him what awaited up in Sally's apartment. He'd make the bastard pay.

The Browning roared once, twice, the muzzle flashes bright in the dim light of the garage.

The first shot missed, whining off the concrete wall behind the man in black and bouncing between the wall and ceiling with a horrendous wail. The second shot connected, right above the other man's left knee. The leg buckled, the man in black falling forward. O'Rourke lined up the sights again, but the man in black started to roll across the aisle, trailing blood, taking cover behind the first vehicle he reached.

A stifled yell of pain echoed through the garage as O'Rourke gained his feet, dashed across to the other side of the aisle to come at his quarry diagonally, and moved along the cars until he saw the man in black's legs partially exposed beside a Vauxhall sedan.

O'Rourke fixed his eyes on those legs as they started to shift, the man in black trying to recover enough to get back in the fight. O'Rourke fired again, working the trig-

ger steadily, sending shots *thunking* into the body of the
car. The back tire exploded and the car sank a little, blood
spattering the neighboring car. The Browning's slide
locked open, and O'Rourke dug a spare mag from inside
his coat and slapped it home. He gripped the gun in both
hands as he crossed the aisle and approached the fallen
man, the growing pool of blood spreading into the aisle an
indication that the man would fight no more.

O'Rourke stood over the body and fired a shot into the
man's head, then another, and one more just because.

He stood for a moment, breathless, part of him wanting to go upstairs and see what remained of Sally, and
the other more tactical side of his mind screaming that
he needed to get away without delay. He listened to the
tactical side. Stowing the Browning, O'Rourke jumped
back into his car and peeled out of the garage, one hand
on the steering wheel, the other dialing Collins on his cell.
They had to get out of Belfast as quickly as possible.

He would have his revenge on Harrison Joule. Later.
After he had the detonators in hand.

CHAPTER NINE

Cars crowded the street and the sidewalks overflowed with pedestrians, some consulting phone maps, others jogging, the remainder walking very fast. Stiletto moved around these human obstacles and made his way to the Embarcadero, a long stretch of two-lane road with trolley tracks down the center of the lanes. On the other side of the road was the bayside walkway that wound around the pier-lined shore.

Crossing the busy street with the crowd, he spotted Cupid's Arrow. The bright yellow bow arced out of the cement, a garden surrounding it, the bowstring (a tube of steel) connecting the two ends.

Stiletto could tell the tourists from the people who lived in the neighborhood. The tourists posed and took pictures in front of the bow. Neighborhood people ignored the monstrosity.

Scott stared at the piece of "artwork" from a short distance, the wind blowing against his face. The cacophony of cars from the Bay Bridge a stone's throw away intruded on his thoughts. What did he do now? The tourists wandered off to the next site on their list. Stiletto walked the circumference of the arrow, feeling stupid. He looked up at the bridge crossing to the other side of the bay. The water shimmered in the sun. Sailboats raced back and forth along the frothy water; larger tankers sailed slowly under the bridge span. The wind rushed with relentless force.

This might have been where William Strong went to meet John Pike, but other than that, what did it mean? There couldn't be any clues here.

A stain on the concrete near the water could have been blood, but there were a lot of stains and gouges in the sidewalk that could have been anything. Besides, Strong hadn't been killed on this spot, so that didn't matter. He turned to stare at the water again, took a deep breath, and cleared his mind of everything but the problem. Okay, Strong's murder hadn't taken place at this location. If the woman in the pictures had one eye on Pike at all times and Johnny couldn't make the scheduled meet, might he have left something for Strong to find?

He started around the circumference again, examining the garden a little closer. Usual dirt. Candy wrappers. Street debris. The flowers bloomed brightly, an explosion of various colors.

And then he saw it—a plastic garden spike. It did not belong. Not there, at least. The dirt was bare.

Stiletto dropped to his knees and used the spike to dig

around the dirt. Somebody jogged by. Nobody paid attention to odd behavior in San Francisco. The city was built on such displays of oddity. The dirt was soft and easy to sift, and he used the spike to move the loose dirt onto the cement.

About an inch down, he found a plastic sandwich bag. *Great, somebody's drug stash.* He tugged the bag loose and a clump of dirt dropped off it as he stood.

OK. Not somebody's drug stash.

Inside the bag was a cell phone. A burner phone, one of those use-it-and-toss prepaid phones. He tore the phone from the bag and pressed the power button. The phone lit up. A rush of adrenaline kicked through Stiletto. Johnny had kept the meeting after all, but Strong had been shot before he could arrive to find the clue.

He pocketed the phone and returned to the hotel.

The discovery called for a drink.

Stiletto took a seat at the hotel bar and ordered a Makers-and-Coke. He sipped the cold liquid and searched through the phone. He checked for pictures first, finding several of an office building that might have been anywhere, but the address was prominent in one picture: two-twenty-one. Another picture showed the street sign for Main Street. He didn't know where the building was, but it wouldn't be hard to find. There had not been any calls made to or from the phone. No stored text messages or notes.

Back in the room, Stiletto used his computer to search for any meaning behind 221 Main Street. He logged into the Trust database to start. DuckDuckGo wasn't going to help this time. He needed to know if any names associated with that address had ever fallen on the radar of law enforcement or the intelligence community. John Pike had taken the pictures for a reason.

He perked up when the search turned up a name.

Oscar DeSoto occupied a suite at 221 Main Street. The fifteenth floor was the headquarters of his architecture firm. Police records showed he had done time in the late '60s for trying to blow up a Marina District police station with a homemade bomb. He'd been part of a radical anti-war group that wanted to take down the establishment using the very means they were opposed to the establishment using. Stiletto shook his head. Yesterday's radicals ran today's establishment; he wondered if they saw the irony. DeSoto had a home address in Marin County, near the coast.

Could mean anything. Stiletto tapped his upper lip. If he went charging after DeSoto and he wasn't who Pike meant for anybody to find, he might face a major problem. But it was the only lead he had.

He paced the room. DeSoto had served time for trying to plant a bomb. Pike's wife and child had been killed by a bomb. Was Pike trying to stop another attack, or had he finally tracked down the one who'd set off the Paris bomb?

Stiletto searched through DeSoto's file. He had still been incarcerated when Pike's family died.

Did he know who planted the bomb?

Stiletto paced again and let the thoughts spin through his head. Pike had meant for William Strong to find the phone. He didn't kill Strong; somebody else pulled the trigger instead. Probably the fashionable female with the diamond-studded purse.

Did it mean Pike had been discovered, and Strong was killed to prevent further information from getting back to the CIA?

He called General Ike and provided an update.

"If Pike is running a rogue operation, he's in deep trouble," General Ike said.

"You're telling me. On both sides."

"I'll mention it to the DCI and see if it will help us keep the dogs at bay a while."

"Anything on the woman?" Stiletto sat on the bed and put his elbows on his knees.

"Nothing yet. We have three very good pictures of her, so we'll find something."

"I have to see DeSoto."

"Be very careful. We have no idea what the connection is."

"Is any help available for me?"

"Beth Carrington is on assignment, and I'm afraid I can't spare anybody else."

"That's okay, sir. I have an idea about who I can call."

"Who might that be?"

"Nikki Fortune."

"I disagree with bringing her into this. Wholeheartedly disagree. Scott, it's a mistake."

"She'll be okay if I tell her it's for me," Stiletto said. "She's outside the box, has her own crew and weapons if needed, and going through her and her father won't strain Trust resources. I can only imagine the big boss won't let me run around forever."

General Ike sighed. "All right. But if she gets out of hand—"

"I will lay a firm hand on her behind, sir."

"That's not what I meant."

"But it *will* work."

Stiletto laughed and ended the call. He made another straight away, catching Nikki Fortune's voicemail. He asked if she might be free to join him in San Francisco for some fun and left a request to call him back. He then looked up 221 Main Street on the computer map and arranged for an Uber driver to pick him up in front of the hotel.

He placed the lunch dishes in the hallway on his exit.

The Uber driver was a young kid with shaggy hair and thick glasses. He had bottles of water in the backseat cup holder for his passengers and told Stiletto he could pick any radio station he wanted. Stiletto told him he liked it quiet and provided the Main Street address. The driver put the Ford Focus in gear and merged into traffic.

The driver didn't talk. Several drivers cut them off for going too slowly, and Stiletto noticed the driver sat on a cushion to better see over the steering wheel. *The kid needs some assertiveness training.*

The driver made a turn onto Howard Street. Potholes dotted the road, and the Ford jolted several times. The buildings on either side of the street showed a depressing gray tinge. A construction crew on the corner was midway through a new steel-and-glass skyscraper. It would stand-out when finished, but for the wrong reason. Everything else in the neighborhood looked old.

The driver turned left onto Main Street and there stood 221 ahead, two other buildings on either side—both similar office structures—and a Greyhound bus station directly across the street. *A gift from the spy gods.* The bus station was the perfect place to sit and watch 221 without anyone noticing he was there.

CHAPTER TEN

Death waited in the hills.

Or, rather, on the slope of the hill leading to the chalet belonging to an international thief, arms dealer, and smuggler named Leon Daschke.

He lay on his belly on the wrap-around balcony in the rear of the chalet, which overlooked a normally peaceful valley in the countryside of Spain. Today it held killers coming for his scalp. He could see them moving up the slope, taking advantage of the natural cover, while he and his men lay in wait. The assault force needed to get a little closer for his shooters to make the best use of their weapons.

Daschke held a Brugger & Thomet MP-9 machine pistol, the stock extended and the magazine stoked with hardball rounds. His men were similarly equipped with a variety of submachine guns since Daschke had access to plenty of hardware from his dealings around the world. He had never intended to use the weapons to defend his life, though. Most of the hardware were samples, to meant to show clients to make sales.

Daschke swallowed hard. His throat was dry—his kingdom for a sip of water.

The brush on the hillside rustled here and there as the attack force moved into position.

What were they waiting for?

And then he heard the helicopter.

He dared not take his eyes off the hillside, though. He could do something about the men in hiding. The chopper, not so much.

It would have been a nice day for a helicopter ride, except Nicole Fortunado, aka Nikki Fortune, needed to clean out a nest of vipers.

She sat close to the left exit as the Huey flew low over the hills in the Spanish countryside. The rolling green hills were very romantically inviting, if only she had a man to bring up here. She had a man with her in the helicopter, Martin Saar, but he was nowhere close to what she wanted in a romantic partner. He was a business partner and a good one. He was also a handy shot with a rifle, which he why he toted a CZ 805 BREN with a fourteen-inch barrel. The 5.56x45mm automatic rifle would get quite a workout.

Nikki carried a pistol in a shoulder harness, an HK45 autoloader that fit her hand like a glove.

She was dressed in commando black despite the sunny day. They had to move on Daschke while he was at the chalet; he often wasn't.

Like Daschke, Nikki Fortune sold weapons, stole stuff, and generally kept every finger and toe dipped in various criminal enterprises. Her father, Primo Fortunado, was the kingpin, but she, his little girl, was quickly taking on more of the responsibilities.

Daschke was one of those crooks who didn't mind stealing from other crooks-in this case, a cache of diamonds from a newly discovered deposit in Russia that wasn't officially being mined. The diamonds would fetch millions on the black market, and Nikki was entitled to those millions because she had stolen them first. Seducing the junior-league smuggler who'd managed to get the sparkly goodness out of Russia had been the easiest part, but then had come Daschke to rain on the parade.

Nikki was partially at fault. She should have been more careful, but she'd carefully tracked Daschke, and now it was payback time. She'd brought an army of mercenaries with her to hammer home the point: *Don't mess with Fortunado.*

Nikki had big plans for those diamonds and the cash they would bring. She was trying to build her own empire separate from her father's, and the stones were a down payment on it. She imagined herself the Queen of the Underworld. Nothing would stop her from obtaining the title.

The chopper swooped over the U-shaped chalet at the top of the hill, and Nikki grinned at the sight on the balcony with its line of defenders ready to repel an attack. She adjusted the mouthpiece of her headset and radioed the pilot.

"Circle around, then use the rockets."

"Yes, ma'am."

From either side of the Huey extended a pair of rocket pods. As soon as the rockets impacted the chalet structure, her commandos would strike.

The chopper circled around, her side dipping low. The ground was close but not so close that she could survive a fall from the cabin. Despite being buckled in, she grabbed her seat tighter.

The chopper leveled off, then the rocket pods flashed, and the cabin filled briefly with smoke as the 20mm rockets closed the gap between the chopper and the house. All four missiles hit hard, orange flames spitting skyward as the blasts rocked the structure.

The pilot aimed for the small courtyard in the chalet's "U," and Nikki and Saar jumped out after they were on the ground. Nikki ripped her HK45 from under her arm as she followed Saar toward the front door.

The chopper lifted away. As the whipping of the rotor blades faded, the crackles of automatic weapons fire intensified.

The fight was on.

Saar stopped in the front doorway. He was Nikki's

height, broad in the chest, with dark hair and a dark mustache, both of which set off his bright blue eyes. He wore black combat fatigues like Nikki, the sleeves of his shirt rolled up and the tattoo on his right arm fully exposed. The ink showed a fish caught on the end of a hook.

Saar kicked open the door and he and Nikki rushed inside, Nikki with the HK45 up in both hands, scanning for any targets.

"Where is it?" Saar said, snapping his head around.

"Down the hall there. To the right!"

Saar went. Nikki followed. The automatic weapons fire was louder now.

She pressed her lips together as she and Saar advanced down the hall.

The fight would end one way or another.

Leon Daschke ignored the fact that his chalet was in the process of burning to the ground.

If he didn't survive today, the fire made no difference.

So, he had to survive.

Commandos came to life on the hillside, their weapons spitting flame as they climbed toward the balcony. Daschke's MP-9 machine pistol bucked against his shoulder as the others joined him in pouring out a heavy salvo. Hot brass from somebody's weapon landed on his neck, but he ignored the burn.

A few of the commandos fell back, tumbling down the

hill, but others did not stop, his bullets seemingly ineffective against their onslaught. And then the wood bottom of the balcony began to splinter around him. Daschke screamed as another type of burn filled his body. His hands stopped working, then his vision went blank, the echoes of the gunfire lasting a second longer before his world became dark and silent.

The gunfire stopped.

Nikki and Saar paused in the doorway of a large study.

"Sounds like it's over," Saar said.

Nikki pushed past him into the room, letting the HK45's muzzle led the way, but then she holstered the pistol.

"Nobody to kill in here."

Saar stayed by the door and didn't sling his rifle. "Hurry."

Nikki nodded and started searching at the corner desk, sorting through drawers, looting various items.

"It's supposed to be here," she said.

"Maybe it was moved."

Nikki checked the wood under the desk, tapping here and there. Nothing but solid knocks answered. With a grunt, she rose, leaned against the desktop, and looked at the paintings hanging in front of the desk.

She didn't want to think about whether the diamonds had been moved. They were somewhere in the house, and her informants had specified the study.

Just not where.

She reached for the painting on the left. Nikki had no interest in art, so she didn't bother looking at what was on the canvas. She removed the painting from the wall. No safe behind it and nothing attached to the back. She placed it on the desk and removed the second painting. She turned it around. The back of this one had something attached to one side of the wooden frame—a black velvet bag that bulged slightly. Nikki smiled.

"Found it."

"Let's go," Saar said from the doorway.

Nikki removed the velvet and opened it. The spark-ly-sparklies were nestled inside, so it was a good day.

Nikki pulled the tie closed and jammed the velvet bag into the side pocket of her fatigue pants. She and Saar joined her strike team that had advanced into the house, where the team leader reported no other hostiles and that they'd lost three.

Nikki wandered out onto the balcony where the line of dead men lay, their fancy automatic rifles now useless, blood dripping through the gaps in the wood boards on the balcony floor. She stopped at Daschke's wrecked body. His eyes remained open. The skin on his face already had the waxen look of the freshly dead. Most of the slugs had struck him in the torso; the large holes in his back, the torn flesh a bright mess of red and pink, testified to many exit wounds. She didn't feel anything. Her mission wasn't personal; there was too much money involved to make it personal. But Leon Daschke had friends who might take his death personally.

Friends who would want to avenge him. Never mind the diamonds. They'd want her head.

She'd be seeing those friends soon enough. The thought of the challenge made her smile. Forget the money; Nikki Fortune loved the rush.

CHAPTER ELEVEN

In a London hotel, Nikki Fortune sat at the table by the window, a gentle breeze blowing through, the sounds of kids splashing in the pool drifting through the screen.

She sat in her bathrobe with a laptop in front of her, answering email. Business didn't stop despite the raid. She still had weapons and equipment to sell. A contact in Israel said they were selling ten F-16s about to go out of service, and did she want them? Nikki replied that she would take six of them and had buyers waiting. She could triple her money if she disassembled the jets and sold the parts. Jet parts of any kind were like gold.

She sat in her pink bathrobe, naked underneath. She was still tired, not only from jet lag but from the raid. Her squad, Saar, and she had taken off in separate directions at the conclusion of the raid, and she was cooling her heels in London for two days before making her way home. Daschke had had friends, which meant *she* had enemies.

She always had enemies. They were a constant in her life.

Nikki answered two more emails before closing down the computer. She left the table, shedding her bathrobe as she finally stepped into the shower. The steamy hot water felt good on her slender frame.

After the shower, she dressed in a loose t-shirt and jeans and clipped a holster to the small of her back, where she slotted the HK45 autoloader. Over the t-shirt, she buttoned a blouse halfway. Room service delivered brunch, and she sat by the window to eat, but first, she opened the drapes full to let in the fresh air. And get a view of the walkway leading to her building.

Nikki was chewing a piece of sausage when she stopped.

Two men walked along the concrete pathway between the pool and the hotel building, and they didn't walk like guests.

They looked like killers—street clothes, blazers, heads moving back and forth in a continuous threat scan. One was white with long blond hair, while the other had a darker tinge to his skin.

Nikki put down her fork, shoved the laptop into a tote bag, grabbed her purse, and decided to hell with everything else. Clothes and makeup were easily replaceable.

Racing down the hall, Nikki stopped short as the elevator opened and the two men stepped out.

The blond said something in a foreign language to his partner, but they both reached under the blazers at the same time.

Nikki flung her purse at the blond. The bag struck him in the face just hard enough to throw him off balance. His right arm came out from under the blazer with a pistol, but he was unable to take aim as he staggered back from the impact. His darker partner had his gun out too, but by then, so did Nikki. The HK45 cracked four times in rapid succession.

Two shots each, center mass, and the killers dropped to the beige carpet and didn't move any longer. Before the ringing in her ears stopped, Nikki was charging down the stairwell, purse recovered, heading for the exit on the ground floor.

She drove casually out of the parking lot behind the wheel of a sensible Mazda sedan. After she caught her breath and made sure there wasn't anybody following her, she reached under the dashboard for a hidden cell phone and dialed Saar.

He answered on the third ring.

"We said no calls for forty-eight hours."

"Two men just tried to kill me."

"Where are you?"

"Driving away from the hotel. Going to need another way out of London. They might be onto me."

"I haven't had any trouble."

Saar was laying low in Berlin.

"Keep your eyes open," Nikki said. "There's a lot at stake here."

"Be careful, Nikki."

She grimaced. "I will. See you soon."

She ended the call and set the phone on the passenger seat.

How did the enemy know where to find her?

She didn't think Saar had an answer, and she didn't know where to start, either. Who else knew she was in London? Had her computer been traced?

The questions would have to wait.

Right now, she had to get out of London.

After she used her cell to alert her father, she listened to a voice message left by Scott Stiletto.

"Would you be available to come to San Francisco? Call me back."

Why yes, she decided. *Yes, I would.*

CHAPTER TWELVE

Harrison Joule wore a grim look as he entered the pub.

News of Lagros' death had saddened him, and now the IRA wanted a sit-down to discuss why Joule sent an assassin to kill some of their guys. Joule wanted to know why the IRA had decided to interfere with his business. If the Irish wanted a war, Joule was ready to accommodate them, personal history be damned.

But for this meeting, he was willing to talk. Perhaps sanity would prevail.

The light inside the pub was dim, matching the night outside, the various shades of wood making up the décor irritating Joule because pub owners refused to try anything different. It looked old and uninviting, but the lack of customers in the middle of the day didn't suggest Joule was among the majority. The flood of customers stood the chance of bursting the seams of the place.

He found his contact in a back corner with a pint in front of him and another pint on the opposite side of the table.

Joule slid into the booth and took a sip of the pint.

"Hello, Harrison," the IRA man said.

The noise within covered their words. Neither would have to speak quietly, which suited Joule perfectly. He wanted to be heard loud and clear when communicating back to the IRA what he expected.

Joule put his elbows on the table and leaned toward the older man. Jimmy Reardon had been an associate of Joule's twenty years ago. It was smart of the current Real IRA bosses to send him to the meeting. They at least had a history. Had they sent one of the younger people so irritating to Joule with the recent difficulties, he might have shot the contact on the spot.

"Jimmy. I'm glad they sent you."

"I bet you are." Reardon chuckled and drank some beer. "I'm here to make sure this doesn't get out of control, Harrison. I'm here to explain a few things."

"Let's hear it, and it better be good. These new kids are trying to rip me off. What am I supposed to do? I had to send my man."

Jimmy Reardon shrugged. "I get it."

"Then let's hear something useful."

Jimmy Reardon took a deep breath. "I have spoken to the army council about this, and they are willing to let you handle the rest of the problem."

"By that, you mean?"

"The IRA will not be upset if you have to deal with the

lads in a violent manner."

"That's rich, Jimmy. Call them off. Tell them to come home."

"They can't, Harrison. That's the problem. The Real IRA isn't trying to steal your detonators. Kevin O'Rourke has his own agenda. He's not working on the orders of the council. That's why he needs your detonators. The council wouldn't allow his little pet project, whatever it is, so he's doing this on his own."

Joule pulled the pint back and took a sip. "I'm listening."

"In a way, we are officially disowning Mr. O'Rourke and his crew."

"After I take care of this problem," Joule said, "I had better not hear any crying from you people."

"There will be none. You have my word."

"You're not with the council any longer, Jimmy. They pulled you out of retirement for this. What loyalty do they have to you?"

"I'd like to think they respect me as an elder statesman. One of the few Republican operators who took the fight to the Brits for years and stayed out of prison."

"Tell them any further trouble after this, and there will be swift retaliation."

"That's exactly what they want to avoid," Reardon said. "It's different now. Not like the old days."

Joule drank half the beer and set the glass back on the table. "It was good to see you, Jimmy."

"You need to come over. Play checkers with me."

Joule smiled as he rose from the booth. "I'm busy for the next few weeks, but we'll see after."

"You were smart, you know."

"What do you mean?"

"To get out when you did, and do what you're doing now. All I do is sit around dreaming of the old days."

"Well," Joule said, "I was always a restless soul. Be seeing you, Jimmy."

Joule walked out of the pub without a look back.

Unlike his old friend, he wasn't thinking about the past. The past was an annoyance. The past was gone. Only the present concerned Harrison Joule, and if the IRA was indeed giving him carte blanche to deal with their renegades, he had to alert Marco Diego straight away.

And tell him to terminate with extreme prejudice should he cross paths with the IRA's "lads."

Buses rumbled in the terminal area, their exhaust fumes filling the air. The fumes tickled Stiletto's nose. He found a bench and sat facing 221 Main. After two hours, the concrete bench became very uncomfortable, but in those two hours, he saw a lot of comings and goings. Mostly office people, all dressed in the latest office fashion. Some clustered on the sidewalk. Those in the clusters were the smokers. They stood near a gated garage that drivers needed a key card to access. The gate stayed up for approximately one minute after each car entered the space.

Accessing the building via the front door was out of the question. Workers flashed passes at the two security guards behind the lobby desk. Visitors without a pass were waved over to check-in, where they acquired a guest badge. Stiletto might go in and say he had an appointment with DeSoto, but if the security guards phoned up to let the office know, his attempted entry would end really quick.

It looked like the garage and the smokers provided the best means of entry, but there would be entrance cameras to avoid. Scott wasn't worried about the cameras. They all had blind spots.

First, he needed appropriate clothes. Second, he needed cigarettes. He didn't like cigarettes. He preferred cigars. In place of cigarettes, he'd find a small stogie, probably a Lonsdale size, that would fit the bill.

He left the bus station.

The cigars were easy enough to find in a smoke shop near the hotel, but the clothes took a little more work. He walked up busy Market Street. The closer he came to a shopping area, the more crowded the streets were—traffic always moving slowly, buses rumbling by, taxis and ride-share cars careening in and out of lanes.

The Westgate Mall sat on the corner of the intersection of Market and 4th Street and stretched twenty stories high. He found a Men's Warehouse that outfitted him with a nice suit and a trio of shirts and ties.

He returned to the hotel with his purchases and ate

dinner in the restaurant while thinking over his plan.

Back in the room, he stretched out on the bed and watched television for a few hours. He didn't mean to doze off in his clothes, but he did.

Stiletto showed up around noon the next day to take advantage of the lunch rush. Several people ate outside the building, sitting on either wooden benches or along the edge of the planters extending from the base of the building. He paid fifteen bucks for his lunch at a sandwich shop around the corner from 221. Between the two slices were an assortment of smoked turkey, ham, and salami, and spicy cheddar cheese with a thin garlic and butter spread, and it tasted very good. He washed it down with mineral water from a glass bottle.

By the time he was finished, a few smokers had ambled over to their spot. Stiletto tossed his trash and lit his cigar, an Espinoza Crème, a very mild blend, in the thin Lonsdale size he'd wanted. It wasn't a fat gangster cigar, but short and thin, so it would blend in with the cigarettes without raising much fuss. He didn't join the conversation within the cluster, instead standing near enough to watch the comings and goings at the garage.

A few cars entered and exited, a horn sounding every time the gate lifted. The gate remained open for sixty seconds exactly. What he'd witnessed yesterday hadn't been a fluke.

Halfway through the cigar, a Mercedes pulled up to the garage, and the driver, who was on his cell phone, reached out with his pass card. The gate howled as it lifted. The driver rolled up his window and eased through. Stiletto tossed the cigar and followed, staying in the car's blind spot, the roofline high enough to also conceal him from the security camera.

The garage had a polished concrete floor, pillars connecting floor to ceiling, with the mailroom and elevators smack in the center. Cars filled every space, and it was a wonder the Mercedes could fit into the only open slot.

Stiletto walked to the back of the garage as if his car were parked there. He found a space between two other cars to squat and hide while the echo of the Mercedes driver's conversation echoed through the cavernous space. After it had faded, Stiletto wondered where DeSoto might park. He'd seen a local paparazzi photo of the architect getting into a black Maserati coupe, but the picture was at least two years old. Did he still have the vehicle? Scott left the hiding spot and roamed in search of the car. He found it parked against the far wall in a reserved spot. He took out another cigar, cut the end, and set fire to the tip. Leaning against the back passenger-side fender, he waited.

For over an hour.

Stiletto's legs hurt from standing on the hard concrete

and leaning against the fender of DeSoto's car only provided a small amount of relief. When a heavyset man in a dark suit emerged from the elevators and started walking to the Maserati, his discomfort faded.

Oscar DeSoto had a full head of hair, and the shirt he wore was properly tailored so as not to stretch against the bulge of his belly. In other words, the buttons weren't straining. He carried the prerequisite briefcase and a topcoat over his arm.

The man continued toward him with a strange look on his face. He was trying to figure out why a man was standing near his car. He finally stopped a few feet away and said, "Get away from my vehicle."

"We need to talk, Mr. DeSoto."

"Make an appointment through my secretary. I cannot stand the unorthodox methods some of you salespeople—"

"Stop it, fatty. I'm not selling anything."

DeSoto blinked.

"We know what you're doing," Scott said. "You'd better consider talking, or you're going away for a long time, and prison isn't what you remember from the '60s. Little rougher now."

DeSoto sucked in a breath.

"You won't end up at some country club minimum-security place either, gramps."

DeSoto stepped close and leaned in. "I don't know what you're talking about. Please remove yourself from my car and be on your way, or I *will* call security."

"Who will do what, exactly? Give me a dirty look? All we want are the names of the people you're working with. Come across, and I go away, and nobody bothers you ever again."

"You're talking nonsense."

"Sure."

DeSoto blinked again. He moved his left foot back half a step. Stiletto smiled. He could read the other man's face clearly. He'd struck a nerve, for sure.

The only flaw in his plan was that he couldn't exit via the gate without a card, and he figured the elevators were operated by the key cards too. When another vehicle entered the garage and the gate horn sounded, he knew it was time to leave while he had the chance.

"We'll be in touch," Scott said. He pushed away from the Maserati and started walking to the exit. He walked like he owned the place. That would leave an impression on DeSoto, as if the confrontation hadn't seared itself into his brain enough already.

Oscar DeSoto watched the man walk away. He glanced at the security cameras, but he had purposely parked in a blind spot because he didn't like being spied on by a bunch of minimum-wage-earning security idiots. The man probably knew that, which was why he wasn't both- ered by waiting for DeSoto to end his workday.

He put his briefcase and coat in the car and dug a cell

phone out of the inside pocket of his blazer. He dialed, and a woman answered. He told her very quickly about what happened.

"You have no idea who this man was?"

"None," DeSoto said. "He didn't identify himself as law enforcement."

"What else did he say?"

"Doesn't matter!" DeSoto's voice echoed in the garage. He quickly climbed behind the wheel and pulled the door shut. "You need to find this man and kill him!"

"I don't take orders from you," the woman on the other end said.

"This is no time for your shit, Elsa," DeSoto said. "We have a problem. *You* need to handle it. *That* is your job."

DeSoto terminated the call without a goodbye. He started the motor, and the rumble of the engine filled the garage. He selected a gear and steered for the exit.

CHAPTER THIRTEEN

DeSoto kept both hands on the wheel but couldn't stop them from shaking.

Who was that man, and what did he know?

He sped onto the Golden Gate Bridge, heading for home in Marin. The waters of the bay extended from beneath the bridge to his left and right. The bay resembled a black abyss in the evening twilight, the rolling fog above the hills ahead a harbinger of death.

DeSoto took a deep breath and tried to calm down. He'd signed on with Harrison Joule, knowing the risks. Knowing the risks, however, was much different than *experiencing* the risks.

He was the president and CEO of DeSoto Industries, in charge of a large materials company that manufactured composite components used in military armaments, mainly guided missiles. His part in Joule's project was concerned with building the bodies of the two missiles Joule planned to sell. He'd arranged for his plant in nearby Oakland to construct the tubes based on specs provided by Joule, telling the plant manager that it was a quiet request from the DOD for something new they were testing. The plant manager didn't argue but requested that the tubes be made after regular production shut down. The plant crew, using high-strength aluminum alloy as requested, had filled four molds, each forming half a tube, then welded the halves together—three days' effort that concluded DeSoto's part in the plan, other than passing the assembled tubes to Elsa Suba and her assistant.

But now somebody had marked him. The FBI? Why hadn't the man identified himself as such? Might he be CIA?

DeSoto wasn't even aware of the other cars or freeway signs. He quickly focused his attention back on the road.

He had met Harrison Joule fifteen years ago while on vacation in the Virgin Islands. They'd hit it off as golfing partners, shared a dislike for "the system," and enjoyed using their fortunes to fund subversive protest groups. DeSoto nearly bragged about his time behind bars for engaging in such efforts in his youth, and the twinkle in Joule's eye had confirmed they were kindred spirits.

Joule had brought him into the group, and DeSoto'd never looked back. When approached about the missile project, he'd pledged his support wholeheartedly, and looked forward to adding his cut of the project to his personal off-shore account.

But now, *the man* had appeared.

He decided that the only way to handle the problem was to use his own men. He'd put the plans in motion as soon as he reached home.

Stiletto sat in the lobby of the Hyatt, reading *Motor Trend* and listening to the music through the overhead speakers. He was in a less-traveled area of the lobby, away from the elevators and doors. He didn't want too many people around when DeSoto's goon squad arrived, which they were sure to do.

If.

If DeSoto was dirty and tied in with William Strong's murder, yeah, he'd send some goons Scott's way. Stiletto hadn't avoided all the cameras at 221, and he'd made sure that any other street cameras and those at the Hyatt had a good shot of him. DeSoto's goons could hack surveillance systems, searching for his image and his location. It might take some time, but they'd find him at the Hyatt.

His seat was next to a window overlooking an outdoor mall adjacent to the Hyatt, and he glanced up now and then to look at the people below, who might have been oversized ants.

He could have called Toby O'Brien and had some FBI men on stand-by, but that would put an operation that was supposed to be off the record very much *on* it, so he didn't do that. Like a hunter attracting prey, he wanted the kills to himself. There would be plenty of time to bring others in when he was one step ahead. This mission wasn't about following the rules. It was about finding out why his friend was on the run and accused of murdering a fellow agent.

Stiletto figured DeSoto would send the usual two goons to brace him. Maybe they'd have orders to kill, and he could at least confirm DeSoto was dirty.

When two men stepped off the lobby escalator from the street entrance, Stiletto knew right away the fight was on. They wore street clothes and heavy coats, too heavy for the outside bay chill. Perfect coats for hiding hardware, though. Scott stayed still. They'd find him. The two men stopped and scanned the lobby. One broke off and went to look at the restaurant area. The other kept his eyes moving. Scott turned a page in the magazine and waited, watching out one corner of his eye. The goon finally spotted him and waved to his partner, who left the restaurant, and the two started their approach.

Stiletto whistled a little tune. He had an exit planned already.

He let them get halfway across the open floor, then set the magazine down and left the chair. He crossed to a stairway door and crashed through, immediately breaking into a fast sprint down the stairs. His shoes clanged on the metal steps, the sound bouncing off the walls. Scott paused on a landing long enough to look back and see the goons following. They shuffled down, one behind the other.

Stiletto raced down the next flight and pushed through another door to the underground garage.

He heard one of the goons talking as the door shut and swung around the corner to press flat against the wall. The goons' footsteps thundered even through the concrete wall. The garage was cold, and Scott zipped up his jacket. He had the .45 under his arm, but he didn't want to use the pistol unless it was absolutely necessary.

When the door swung open, he waited. One goon stepped into the garage with a gun in his hand. Stiletto let the second man enter as well. The second man's hands were empty. Scott struck like a cornered cat, aiming his attack at the second thug. The man let out a yelp as Stiletto wrapped his arms around his neck, using his body for leverage as he launched his legs at the other goon. Stiletto's legs extended like two steel rods, connecting with the first goon's chin. He shuffled back and went down, the gun skidding away. Stiletto swung his weight against the second man and pinned him to the ground, snaking a hand under his jacket to grab the automatic pistol holstered there. It was a polymer gun, a Smith & Wesson M&P, so bashing him over the head would only hurt the gun. He grabbed him by his shaggy hair, lifted his head, and bashed his skull into the concrete instead.

As he rolled off the goon, the other one went for his gun. Scott wouldn't reach him in time. He had to shoot first. Scott swung up the S&W and fired once. Flame flashed from the muzzle, and the goon's left elbow exploded in a burst of blood and torn flesh. His scream filled the cavernous garage, joining the echo of the gun blast.

CHAPTER FOURTEEN

Stiletto leapt to his feet at the sound of screeching tires. An SUV rolled toward him, a man with a submachine gun leaning out the passenger window. As the vehicle stopped, Stiletto dove forward and somersaulted for cover. The submachine gun lit up the garage, rounds chewing into the concrete wall and ricocheting everywhere. Light fixtures shattered, car windows broke, and bullets tore into vehicle bodies. Stiletto stopped behind a support pillar, extended the S&W around, and let off a trio of rounds. The submachine gun stopped. Doors opened and closed.

Stiletto swallowed. Well. This might be a little tougher than he thought. He rose to his feet, sliding back up the side of the pillar.

He fired around one side, then the other since the goons had spread out. Stiletto ran forward, slid over the hood of a car directly in front of him, and then ran crouched over in front of the neighboring vehicles, staying near the bumpers. Weapons barked, rounds tearing into the cars and nipping at his heels. Stiletto dived between a truck and a van, extended his arm from underneath the front of the van, and shot a goon in the foot. He howled as he tried to stay upright, but he eventually crashed headfirst. Stiletto fired again and split his head open.

The rest of the shooters stayed low, allowing Scott precious seconds to get up and run across the aisle to the other row of cars. He dropped to the floor and crawled across the oil-stained ground between vehicles to reach the aisle straight ahead. From there, it was a left turn and a sprint for the exit. More shouting erupted behind him as the goons figured out the plan. At least *they* had a plan. He had to get out of there. So much for making them talk, but he now knew DeSoto was the man to see. Whatever he was doing, Scott had spooked him enough for the murder attempt.

Did he know where John Pike was?

Stiletto cleared the opposite aisle and started running, the gunmen racing to catch up. He fired two rounds over his shoulder, and the pistol's action locked back over the now-empty magazine. He tossed the gun. Time for the Colt Combat Government.

The SUV joined the chase, the gunmen moving aside to give it room. The headlights blazed behind Scott, his forward shadow stretching across the floor to the exit and the street and—what? Safety? Certainly not. Only uncertainty lay ahead.

He should have called O'Brien and the FBI.

Scott took out his Colt .45 autoloader, clicking off the safety, and ran faster, legs burning, as the SUV closed the gap.

A sedan sped through the entryway, its headlights flashing into Scott's eyes. He kept running. The car screeched to a stop, the driver twisting the car so the passenger side faced him, blocking the way. The face of the woman behind the wheel made Stiletto stop short. The woman shouted, "Down!" as she swung up a stainless-steel pistol. Stiletto hit the ground hard, and the gun roared three times. Stiletto felt the bullets whistle overhead as he looked back. The SUV's windshield caved in, the driver's face exploding in a flash of red, and the vehicle careened to the left to smash into a pillar. The impact made the ground shake as the hood and bumper crumpled.

Stiletto faced forward. He wanted to laugh. *She could have at least returned my call first.*

"You're gonna get killed if you stay there!" the dark-haired woman with the equally dark eyes shouted.

This was not an illusion. Neither were the goons still charging their way. Stiletto bolted for the sedan, wrenching open the passenger door and diving inside.

CHAPTER FIFTEEN

Nikki Fortune had a smile on her face as she floored the accelerator pedal. She swung the car back around to the exit before Stiletto had the door shut, and the force of the forward movement forced the door closed, Stiletto pulling the remainder of his right leg inside just in time.

"Dammit, Nikki!"

She laughed and made a sharp right turn onto the street, the tires screeching and the engine racing as she swung in and out of lanes to put as much distance behind them and the Hyatt as possible.

"Buckle up," Nikki Fortune said. "It's the law."

Stiletto sat up and clicked his seatbelt. "I'm beginning to think my boss was right!"

"What did he say?"

"Calling you wasn't a good idea."

"But you did."

"Because I need help and there isn't anybody else."

"Gee, thanks. I'm the last resort?"

"You're sure as hell entertaining."

She laughed again. He glanced at her. Her lips were pulled back, the smile genuine, her dark eyes bright. She loved the action. Nikki Fortune was having the time of her life.

"How'd you find me?" he said.

"You're like following a bouncing ball."

"How long have you been here?"

"Long enough."

She made a turn onto the southbound 101 freeway and merged with traffic. Her right foot finally lifted off the gas pedal, and they matched the speed of the other cars on the freeway.

"Where are we going?"

"My hotel near the airport. The Hyatt might be a little hot for a while."

"I have stuff back in my room that I need."

"We can't go back, Scott."

"There's a computer I need."

"Let's get you secured, and then I'll go back for it."

"That should be fun."

"They won't be expecting a woman to show up. This is not up for discussion."

"Who's arguing? You think I'm a green rookie?"

"Based on how easy it was to catch up with you, yeah."

"Bitch."

"Idiot."

Brake lights flashed red ahead. Nikki slowed down,

then stopped. Traffic didn't move.

"Who was chasing you?" she said.

Stiletto explained about his attempt to stir Oscar DeSoto into reacting to the garage confrontation.

"I'd say he reacted, all right," Nikki said. Traffic started moving, but slowly. Presently they passed a crash on the right shoulder, and speed picked up again.

"I wanted to grab one to question, but I wasn't expecting a triple gun crew."

"I'd say this DeSoto fellow wants you very dead."

"Which means there's much more going on than we originally thought."

"What exactly *is* going on?"

Stiletto realized she didn't know the whole story. If she was going to be of use, he had to tell her everything. Since he wasn't on an official mission, there was nothing classified to worry about. He'd have thrown the rule book out anyway. If he couldn't trust Nikki Fortune, daughter of the boss of one of the biggest mafia syndicates in Europe, who *could* he trust?

He explained about the murder of William Strong, the connection with his pal John Pike, and how he was trying to come up with answers before the CIA issued a termination order.

"The CIA again?" she said. "Do they stand around figuring out how to be jerks?"

"You might be surprised," Stiletto said.

"Even my father would want to talk to Pike in this case

to find out why he took off on his own."

"The CIA has a lot to hide."

"Don't we all?"

Stiletto agreed. "Unfortunately."

"And what are *you* hiding?"

He glanced at her. She had a half-grin and a gleam in her eyes. *She's not serious.*

"When we get to the hotel," he said, "maybe I'll show you."

"I have to get your computer first. Then will you show me?"

"If I'm in the mood, sure."

"Oh, you'll be in the mood, all right."

Staying on 101 south, Nikki Fortune turned off the freeway as they approached San Francisco International Airport. Stiletto made a joke about having seen the airport already. She drove to the neighboring Hilton hotel, although calling it "neighboring" was a bit of a stretch. A few blocks separated the hotel from the airport, but there was a view of the bay, and if you had a room facing the airport, you could watch the airplanes take off.

Nikki said her room faced the freeway.

Typical.

The elevator brought them to her floor, and she unlocked the door. The lights were already on, including the bathroom light. The drapes were closed, and her suitcases were stacked on the bed nearest the window. There were two beds with a nightstand between them.

"Did you even unpack?" Stiletto said.

"No."

"What's with the lights?"

"Well," she said, turning to face him, "let's say I left London in a bit of a hurry."

"Somebody's after you?"

"I think so."

"For what?"

"I killed a guy to steal back what he stole from me, and his gang is trying to get even."

Stiletto laughed. "That's rich," he said. "No wonder you flew out here so fast."

"If I'm not safe with you," she said, "I'm not safe anywhere."

"I gotta hear this one," he said. "It'll be a hoot. How does anybody steal *anything* from you?"

"I have to go."

She started past him.

He blocked her way by holding up an arm.

"You don't get away that easy."

"Move," she said, "or I will punch you in the solar plexus."

"Then I won't be in any shape to show you what I'm hiding."

She folded her arms. "Touché."

Stiletto opened the door for her. "Computer, clothes,

basically everything."

"Room key?"

He fetched the key card from his wallet. She stuck it in the left cup of her bra.

"Dammit, Nikki!"

"Be right back."

"Your left boob looks funny."

"I've heard that before."

"What am I supposed to do while you're gone?"

"Mini fridge in the corner. Have a beer. Remote's on the nightstand."

She breezed past him, going by so quickly that a trail of black hair brushed his left arm. Stiletto grinned and shut the door, then beelined for the mini-fridge. He was going to select more than a beer.

CHAPTER SIXTEEN

The first thing Nikki Fortune had to do was ditch the car.

She should have done it before going back to her hotel, but sometimes you could bend the rules a little.

She traveled north on the 101 heading back to San Francisco and pulled off at the Candlestick Exit, the famed ballpark long gone and replaced by a condo development. She steered the sedan around one of the construction sites and parked on the curb. From there, she walked to a spot between two half-finished buildings where another car, this one a nice Chevy Impala, waited. She started the motor and made her way back to the freeway. She'd hidden the car shortly after her arrival seventy-two hours before.

It was the kind of detail embedded in spies and criminals. It wasn't foolproof, but ninety—nine percent of the time, it kept you alive and off the radar.

She drove the Impala back into San Francisco and to the Hyatt. She had to park two blocks away because of so many police cars on the street. She couldn't help but laugh. Stiletto had caused a ruckus indeed.

She had no gun of her own, and Stiletto's room card gave her access to the only hotel entrance the police weren't blocking, but it still had some officers stationed by to screen guests.

Her heart rate was still elevated as she rode up to Stiletto's floor. Getting his gear out and getting past the cops, along with any stray killers still hanging around, gave her quite the shot of adrenaline. She'd made the right choice getting out of London and coming to the United States.

The rush was better than the money.

She reached Stiletto's room and used the key card to open the door. She stepped into the dark room and let the door shut behind her. Moving forward, she passed the bathroom and flipped a light switch, and the lamps brightened the room.

There was a shuffle behind her, and the cold muzzle of a gun touched her neck.

Nikki raised her hands.

She heard the man behind her swallow.

"You're hesitating," Nikki Fortune said, "because you weren't expecting a woman, right?"

She dropped her hands and spun, slamming a fist into the man's gut. The man let out a howl and doubled over, and Nikki brought a knee into his face. His nose crunched under the solid blow from her kneecap, and he dropped. She patted him down for identification or a cell phone but found nothing. Another dead end for Scott. Oh, well.

She quickly packed his luggage, not bothering to fold anything, jamming loose items into the suitcase. She left the business suit hanging. He wouldn't need it again. She grabbed the laptop and other gear she knew he'd need and hustled out. She had to step over the unconscious goon to get to the door but faced no other complications.

It was time to get back to the Hilton and see what Stiletto was hiding in his jeans.

Elsewhere in the city, the next morning, an older man and a younger woman awoke in a room in the Palace Hotel, off New Montgomery Street. The old-style building had been particularly attractive to the man. His name was John Pike.

Plus, it was far away from the Hyatt and where William Strong had wanted to meet. As Pike lay in bed, the woman beside him stirring, he wondered if the cell phone had been found.

He knew Billy was dead. The woman had told him so. She'd spotted Billy following them, doubled back on his trail, and shot him when the opportunity arose. There had been no chance for Pike to sound a warning, and he felt the weight of responsibility. But perhaps Billy had communicated with headquarters before she caught up with him.

Pike intended to add Billy's murder to the account he'd soon settle.

The woman stretched, long legs pushing at the covers, her long arms touching the headboard. Elsa Suba let out a satisfied sigh and turned to Pike.

"Sleep well, darling?"

Her words were dusted with a Hungarian accent.

"Fine," he said. His voice was a little gravelly. His hair was gray and messed up.

"Why are you lying still?"

"Back hurts."

"You're so old."

"Happens to all of us. Eventually."

He wasn't old-old. Fifty-eight. He still had his hair, unlike some of his colleagues. He didn't feel old. His head told him he was still eighteen, but his body often disagreed—the hard way.

Presently, he eased out of bed with a grunt and grabbed his robe from the floor, throwing it over his naked body. He might be older, but not everything was sore, and some of it still worked relatively well.

Elsa stretched again, grinning at him. There were thirty years between them, easily. She wouldn't tell him her age. All he knew was the woman had an animal attraction to him, and he'd decided to use it to his advantage.

She had long blonde hair, the prerequisite blue eyes, a curvy figure, and a small scar on the lower left side of her jaw. She wasn't some skinny Minnie who would fly away in the wind. She had enough mass that Pike could fall on top of her and not wonder right after if he'd cracked a rib.

She could run fast, shoot straight, and knew how to plant a bomb. In other words, she was the perfect woman if you were an international terrorist.

Or pretending to be one.

"You shower first," she said. "I'll get the coffee going."

He nodded and headed for the bathroom.

As he lathered his face with shaving cream and started scraping off whiskers, he couldn't help but notice what looked like extra gray in his hair. The stress of the last few weeks was getting to him. Billy Strong's discovery of him and Elsa had spiked his blood pressure a few notches, and with Billy dead, the CIA would have a lot of questions for him. He was taking a huge risk by not finding a way to report to headquarters, but this mission was personal.

He hated that he was causing friends and colleagues in the Special Activities Division pain, but to stop and explain what he was doing might result in being ordered to stand down. In fact, there was no doubt in Pike's mind that he'd have been ordered not to go. If he was caught and his true identity somehow exposed, the CIA's entire covert apparatus would be in jeopardy. This was the best chance he'd ever had of catching up with Harrison Joule. He was taking a big risk, yes, but a worthy one.

In all the years spent searching for his family's killer, the only thing he'd ever been able to dig up was a name. Harrison Joule was a ghost he chased in his dreams, and real life wasn't much different. And now, thanks to an informant who knew Joule needed outside assistance with a job, he'd eventually come face to face with the man who'd set off the bomb in Paris that destroyed his life. But the mission required certain compromises. He had to follow the trail to the end and see for himself.

Pike had quickly visited his bank, where he'd removed the appropriate "John Chambers" cover identity documents from a safe deposit box, then attended the introductory meeting, where his informant had put Pike and Elsa together. She'd believed his background, and given the authority to hire the extra hand by her boss, she'd agreed to hire Pike.

The CIA would be sending somebody after him, he knew, especially after what had happened to Billy Strong, but if they started where Billy fell, they might find the clue he'd left behind to put them on the right track.

He again wondered what Elsa saw in him. She could have her pick of any number of much younger men. Why him? He grinned. Why question it? She was the perfect insider. Because of her, the upper levels of the Joule organization wouldn't question him or why he'd wanted to join the outfit.

He stepped under the shower and had started soaping up when the curtain moved aside and one long, shapely leg entered the tub, followed by the rest of Elsa in her busty and curvy glory.

"You might use all the hot water," she said, stepping forward to take the soap from his hands.

CHAPTER SEVENTEEN

After their shower, Pike handed her a mug of coffee as she finished dressing. He refused to have the coffee sent up. He had a portable percolator on the dresser with his favorite beans. Good coffee was one luxury he didn't like to go without. They both wore street clothes and tennis shoes. They sat by the window. Elsa sipped her coffee and scrolled through her phone.

"They missed," she said.

Pike swallowed some hot coffee. "What?"

"DeSoto's hit team. The man got away."

Pike took another drink.

Elsa sighed. "Well, DeSoto has outlived his usefulness. If the Feds are onto him, there's only one thing we can do."

"Do we have time?"

"We'll have to split up." She put the phone down. "You go on ahead and deliver the tubes. I'll take care of DeSoto and catch up with you."

"I don't know if I like that."

"They aren't going to pick on you, John." She laughed.

"Well, I don't know them, they don't know me."

"I've vouched for you. That's all they need."

He smiled at her. The lies came so easily. He reached across the table for her hand and gave it a squeeze. "You are the best thing that's ever happened to me."

She smiled back. "Me too. But sometimes duty calls, right?"

"Of course." He withdrew his hand.

"I'm glad we had this morning," she said.

He grinned.

Elsa made an appointment by phone to see DeSoto. He said he'd be at his home in Marin. She left after lunch, giving Pike a lingering good-bye kiss. He packed their bags and used the menu on the television to check out. A bellboy would be up to take their belongings to the cab he'd ordered. While he waited, he placed a large stain-less-steel trunk on the bed and flipped up the latches. Raising the lid, he looked inside.

Two matte-black tubes lay side by side, packed in foam. They were open only at the back end. The front was pointed, like a missile's. Pike ran a hand down the length of one tube. He didn't like what he assumed these missile tubes were to be used for.

He'd been undercover many times in his life, and this

time was only different because he had no cavalry standing by. No contact with home base.

Except through the cell phone he'd left for Billy. He took out his phone to send a message but stopped when somebody knocked on the door—the bellboy. Pike opened the door and helped the young man load their bags on the rolling cart.

"Are you sure he'll be at the house?" Nikki said.

"After his goons failed to kill me, you bet," Stiletto said.

Scott steered Nikki's rented Chevy up a winding two-lane road, following the instructions of the in-dash GPS unit. Rolling hills of brown surrounded them. California was in the middle of a very bad drought. There were patches of green, but nothing like the scenery would have been had the land been properly watered. McMansions sprouted out of the ground every mile or two, sprawling estates usually surrounded by ornate fences. Some of the homes had horses roaming about.

At least the sky was blue and clear, and every now and then, Scott could look left and see the ocean. The red towers of the Golden Gate Bridge also peek-a-booed over the hills.

Stiletto made a right turn and accelerated up an inclined road. As they reached the summit, a steel gate barred further travel. A sign read PRIVATE PROPERTY.

TRESPASSERS WILL BE PROSECUTED, but some joker had spray-painted over "Prosecuted" and written "Tarred and Glittered" instead. Stiletto said, "New version of tarred and feathered?"

"It *is* San Francisco," Nikki said. "Good thing I'm wearing anti-glitter underwear."

Stiletto let out a chuckle. He shifted to reverse and backed down the hill, pulling into a cluster of trees and nosing the vehicle as far off the road as he could. When he finally stopped, the front end of the Impala dipped a little with the slope of the ground.

They left the car and started hiking along the slope of the hill, trudging through the dry grass, snapping dryer twigs. The trees provided some cover, but not the kind they wanted. They followed another rise to a hill overlooking the DeSoto property. Stiletto dropped flat and took a pair of binoculars from under his jacket. Nikki left about eight inches between them and got on her stomach. A tree provided partial shade. They were close enough to see and probably be seen, but DeSoto had nowhere to go from here.

The perimeter fence ringing the property was steel, painted black, with trees on the opposite side. The foliage blocked much of the grounds, but Stiletto identified a large pool and patio in the rear and a multiple-story house, windows reflecting the sunlight. In front was a circular driveway, marble columns holding up the overhang of the porch. The front door was dark red. There were two or three figures on the grounds moving about, and Stiletto thought they were armed.

"What do you see?"

"Three armed troops so far," he said. "Pistols on their hips. Street clothes. Might be more inside."

"Is he expecting somebody, or is this the usual cadre?"

"You'd have to ask him."

The sound of a motor reached their ears at the same time. Scott swung the binoculars to the left. "Uh-oh," he said.

"What?"

He handed her the glasses. She zeroed in on the car and especially the driver, the blonde hair a sure sign of her identity.

"The woman who was with your friend?" Nikki said.

Scott took back the binoculars. "She stopped at the gate and opened it herself."

"How liberated of her."

"Now she's driving up the access road. The trees are in my way."

The blonde woman parked her car in front of the house. Two of the guards made their way to her. If there was talking, Stiletto and Nikki were too far away to hear it.

The blonde raised her right hand.

"She has a weapon," Stiletto said.

"Oh, no."

Automatic fire crackled from the weapon in the woman's hand, and one guard went down. She shifted her aim and shot the next one, then she raced around the front of the car, blasted the locks on the front door, and stormed inside. Pistol shots barked. Automatic fire answered. Then the wind carried away the sound of gunfire.

Stiletto jumped up and started running down the hill.

"Scott!"

Stiletto ran faster, kicking up a cloud of dust, ducking the low branches stabbing at his face. He hauled out his Colt .45. The woman had the answers he needed, and he was going to get those answers, or else.

Nikki shouted, "Wait for me!"

Elsa Suba pushed the gate open and returned to her car. Before she started forward, she grabbed the Uzi pistol from her purse and snapped back the action. The weapon was a scaled-down version of the Israeli submachine gun, a very handy if top-heavy shooter, and she'd had it over fifteen years. The matte-black steel was scuffed and scratched, but the gun had never failed her, and she knew it wouldn't fail her now.

She drove the car to the front of the house, and as she started around the curving driveway, two of DeSoto's men started their approach. She was not a stranger to them. They might be surprised by her unscheduled visit, but neither would be expecting trouble.

Elsa stepped out of the car.

"We weren't expecting to see you today," said the nearest guard.

Elsa didn't bother to reply. She brought up the mini-Uzi. The face of the guard a mere ten yards away blanched as she squeezed the trigger. Flame flashed from the muzzle, and the slugs cut the man down. Elsa shifted her aim. Her next burst struck the other man's chest as he went for his gun. He hit the ground a little harder than his partner had.

Elsa moved quickly. There would be two more inside. Up the front steps. She fired into the lock, the wood splintering, the steel knob and deadbolt falling out. Inside and across the tiled entryway. Curving staircase to her right, rooms left. An armed man in a doorway. He fired once. The shot whistled over her shoulder and smacked into the wall behind. She triggered the Uzi and wiped out the man and part of the doorway. Dropping the now-empty magazine, she reloaded and started up the staircase, her tennis shoes making quiet thuds on the carpeted stairs. She kept her head low, and when the last guard appeared on the landing, his handgun speaking twice, the rounds parted her hair. She was glad she hadn't gone for a permanent. She raised her weapon and stitched him crotch to chin, leaping over his body when she reached the second floor.

She walked calmly down the hall to the last door on the left, her hair bouncing on her shoulders and tickling her neck. She smiled. This was easier than she'd thought it would be. One last target and she could rejoin John and get back to what they did best. She stepped through and raised her weapon once more.

"Hello, Oscar," she said.

CHAPTER EIGHTEEN

"What are you doing?" DeSoto shouted. "Wait!"

Elsa squeezed the trigger. Flame licked from the muzzle, and DeSoto's body hit the carpet with a wet *thunk*.

Elsa dropped the weapon into her purse and went behind the desk, careful not to step in any blood or touch the body. The CPU of DeSoto's desktop unit sat under the desk. She inserted a USB thumb drive into one of the ports. The screen brightened and announced the new device had been found. She opened the lone folder on the driver and clicked a .EXE file. Presently the virus on the USB transferred to DeSoto's hard drive and ate everything on it. If the machine was connected to other computers or had a link to his corporate network, the virus would spread there too. Anything DeSoto had on the project would be long gone before anybody discovered the body.

Elsa Suba hustled out the way she'd arrived.

Stiletto coughed as some of the dust he kicked up went into his mouth and nose.

But he didn't stop. He reached the gate, vaulted over it, and continued onto the estate. Nikki Fortune followed, the impact of the landing jolting up her calves when her feet hit the hard ground. She took out her pistol and kept after Scott, grateful for her daily five-mile morning jog.

She didn't try to overtake Scott. She had no chance. The man was on autopilot, singularly focused, and Nikki hoped she could keep him from making the unavoidable mistakes sure to come with that kind of tunnel vision.

Stiletto reached the assassin's car as the woman exited the front door. The killer froze in the doorway, but only for a moment. She grabbed an Uzi from her purse. Stiletto ducked and rolled as Uzi rounds cut into the dirt. He reached a hedge and dived over. The assassin tracked him with the Uzi, firing again.

Nikki stopped and took a two-handed grip on her pistol. She fired once. A chunk of the front door exploded and pelted the woman in the face. She pivoted and fired, but Nikki was already somersaulting forward. She came up on her stomach and fired again. She let another shot go, but the assassin wasn't in the doorway anymore. The woman slid across the hood of her car, cooking off the rest of the Uzi's magazine. Nikki rolled again as the ground exploded around her.

The woman jumped into her car and peeled out of the driveway. Bits of gravel flew into the air, and the exhaust was an odorous thwack straight up Nikki's nose.

Stiletto rose from behind the hedge and tracked the car with the Colt Combat Government, firing once, twice, a third time. One .45 ACP hollow-point struck the trunk, the other the upper corner of the back windshield, neither impact doing any worthwhile damage to the escaping vehicle or the killer behind the wheel.

When metal screamed and crashed, he knew she'd plowed through the gate.

Nikki, back on her feet, yelled, "Come on!"

Stiletto slapped a new magazine into the Colt and sprinted after Nikki this time, his face locked in an annoyed grimace.

Maybe there was still a chance to catch the killer.

"Go faster!"

Stiletto grunted as he spun the wheel left, right, left, to track the winding road. No sign of the woman's car. He had no idea what kind of lead she had, but she couldn't go stupid-fast. The conditions of the road wouldn't allow that. Even an expert had to stay within a certain limit.

"There she is!"

The woman's car appeared as they cleared a bend, disappearing again, then reappearing as Stiletto followed the road.

Nikki checked the chamber of her pistol and powered down her window. "Get close enough, and I'll blast her tires."

"Good luck."

She gave him a glare he didn't see, his eyes on the road, his strong hands working the wheel. Finally, a straight. Nikki's head whipped back as he accelerated. She leaned halfway out the window and tried to steady her Glock-19, the wind slamming against her and forcing the muzzle to move where she didn't want. Her hair trailed behind her, strands in her face, and she had to hold onto the car with her free hand, so clearing the hair wasn't an option. She aimed as best as she could and fired. One shot. Another. A third. No visible impact on the car in front of them. Nikki dropped back inside as the road curved again.

"Get close again," she said.

Stiletto's hands tightened on the wheel. They made another turn, and the ocean appeared on the right-hand side, the Golden Gate Bridge ahead. The woman swung into a pullout, kicking up a shower of rocks and a cloud of dust. Stiletto slammed the brakes, tires screeching, the car coming to a stop in the middle of the road as the woman steadied the Uzi out the driver's side window.

Nikki screamed.

Stiletto threw the shifter into reverse and floored the pedal. Flame flashed from the mini-Uzi, rounds stitching into the hood as the car rushed backward, Stiletto craning his head to look out the rear window. He stopped again before the last curve.

"Go go go!" Nikki shouted, bracing her gun on the top of the door.

Stiletto accelerated forward, but when they reached the pullout, the woman's car was gone. Stiletto cursed. He continued following the road as it wound toward the 101 freeway, but the assassin was gone.

They continued to the 101. When they joined the traffic on the freeway, they cruised across the Golden Gate Bridge. Neither spoke.

Stiletto finally had to loosen his jaw after mashing his teeth together. A good lead had slipped away.

And with her, any information he might have picked up on John.

CHAPTER NINETEEN

Marco Diego was your typical charming sex-on-a-stick Latin male, with a lean and well-muscled body and thick black hair. He could usually have any woman he wanted. All he had to do was make eye contact and smile. But that trick had not ever, not in the four times he'd attempted it, worked on Elsa Suba. But she had fallen for the old guy standing in front of him, who had some gray hair and was starting to come out in the middle? He didn't get it. The woman was crazy.

He met John Pike in the baggage terminal at the Rio de Janeiro airport and firmly shook his hand, introducing himself and taking his carry-on.

Pike said, "You don't have to."

"It's my pleasure, *mi amigo.* Welcome," he replied.

Pike had not taken a commercial flight, but a private charter arranged by Diego. He cleared Customs without trouble, but the Customs agents also needed to inspect the plane, so none of the luggage could be off-loaded until they'd finished.

They started through the busy Rio airport and outside to a chauffeured sedan. You could cut the humidity with a knife. Diego was used to it, however. Pike wiped his forehead and neck several times as they moved forward. Male and female voices, not only in the native language but several others from around the world, broadcasted announcements over loudspeakers. The high volume battered Diego's ears, and judging by the wince Pike made at each blaring voice, bothered him as well.

A melting pot of tourists crowded the outside of the terminal, jostling for cabs, loaded with bags, some equally loaded with kids as Diego loaded the carry-on and case into the trunk of the sedan. They were parked curbside away from the crush of people, but stragglers drifted their way all the same.

Diego allowed Pike to get into the car first.

"The flight was okay?" Diego buckled his seat belt. The plush leather seats were quite fine, and the big Lincoln was crisply air-conditioned.

"It was very good if a bit lonely. Will it go back for Elsa?"

"She'll have to fly like a regular person, I'm afraid."

"I don't know if she'll like that."

The driver left the curb and drove around the perimeter of the airport to a private gate. After punching in a code to raise the gate, the driver cruised to the hanger, where the jet and customs agents waited. Presently the plane was signed off, and the driver transferred Pike's and Elsa's luggage from the jet to the trunk of the sedan.

After a while, they merged with traffic on the highway.

"Ever been to Rio?" Diego asked.

"Never."

"It looks better on television. Don't bother trying to see much through these tinted windows. You'll have quite a view from your hotel, but like I said…"

"A lot of things are better on television," Pike said.

Diego laughed.

He didn't need to pull one of those "Do you know who I am?" routines. Almost everybody knew Marco Diego. Three Western governments wanted his head. Some of the others hired him now and again to wage a proxy battle against their enemies. The fact that he was a wanted man upped his demand, oddly enough, and Diego charged a high premium for his services.

"Elsa has told me a lot about you," Diego said.

"The good stuff, I hope."

"She says you're lousy in bed."

It was Pike's turn to laugh.

"What's so funny?"

"She won't respond to you, which you can't stand, and you're stunned she's responded to me."

Diego flashed an embarrassed smile. "You caught me."

"I don't get it either, but she's a wonderful woman."

"Maybe that's the difference," Diego said. "I'm not interested in how wonderful she is."

"You only wanted her for carnal reasons."

"Didn't you?"

"Not at first. She's young enough to be—"

"What?"

"My daughter."

Diego laughed again. "I think we will get along fine, *mi amigo.* We're going to your hotel, a very nice one overlooking the beach."

"Are you staying there?"

"Good heavens, no. I have a safe house. Not even you or Elsa can know where I am."

"Understandable."

"You'll keep the tubes until I call for you. Tomorrow morning. We'll give Elsa time to get here and rest a little before the next leg."

"Where are we going next?"

Diego smiled. "Relax, *mi amigo.* Leave all the details to me."

John Pike knew all about Marco Diego.

Both the United States and Britain wanted Diego's head, and two years earlier, Pike had coordinated with a team of MI6 agents to try to set a trap for Diego in Nice. An informant had said he'd be traveling through Nice on his way north. The agents had spread out along the main roads, airports, and other transportation hubs, ready to pounce, but the terrorist had never shown up. Either he'd been tipped off, or worse, decided not to pass through after all.

Pike didn't know how many people Diego had killed, but most of them were military and government officials who had somehow crossed his gunsights. He killed for money. There was no ideology behind his sniper's scope, car bomb, or whatever other machinery of death he employed. On the one hand, the non-ideological terrorist could be turned. He was no more loyal to a mission or employer than the length of his neck.

On the other hand, killers like Diego didn't fit the fanatic role. They could not be analyzed that way. He wasn't crazy; he was simply a man doing a job. For Pike, he was a means to an end, a stepping stone to be used. If everything went his way, Pike would soon put a bullet in Diego's head and end the killer's work for good. He cared not one bit for the credit of such a kill. All he wanted was Harrison Joule, the man Diego worked for. The man who had planted the bomb that killed his wife and his unborn daughter. Everyone else was collateral damage.

Pike watched the man talk. Rio not as good in real life as on TV? Whatever. They were the empty words of a man living on borrowed time who thought he was in the presence of a compatriot just as mercenary as he was. He could brag about a secret safe house all day, but Diego had no clue about how truly *unsafe* he really was.

It wasn't impossible to see out the tinted windows, and John Pike caught glimpses of beach activity and a very busy street—nothing he hadn't seen before in a hundred other places. Pike let out a breath. He'd been around the world so many times, nothing impressed him anymore. If he survived this mission, if he didn't get fired and lose his retirement, it was probably time to get out of the game. He couldn't imagine a better mission on which to exit.

And while Diego thought it was funny Elsa was old enough to be Pike's daughter, Pike didn't see anything funny there. Not because the relationship would have been inappropriate under normal circumstances, but because he was reminded about the reason for his mission.

She probably was old enough to be his daughter, had his daughter lived.

CHAPTER TWENTY

Diego used the key card to unlock the hotel room. He pushed the door open with a flourish as Pike entered, and the bellboy carried the luggage into the room. Diego tipped the bellboy, who left them alone, closing the door softly behind him.

"Let me see the prize we worked so hard for," Diego said, taking the stainless-steel case and placing it on the king-sized bed.

"Are you aware—"

"About DeSoto? Yes, yes. Ah-ha. Here we are. Very nice workmanship, don't you think?" He traced his fingertips over one of the tubes. "They will look much better once they're fully assembled."

Diego closed the case.

"You don't need to think about that right now. Right now, you need a shower, maybe a drink, and time to unwind from the flight. Elsa will be here in a few hours."

Diego pulled Pike into a brief embrace, patting his

back. "Good to finally meet you, *mi amigo.* We will work well together."

He left the room.

Pike stared at the door after it had clicked shut. He surveyed the room cautiously. It had been booked well in advance. The place could be clean of surveillance, or it could be loaded with cameras and sound equipment. He was an unknown, brought into the project by Elsa and approved by Harrison Joule without ever seeing the big boss. Diego had every right to be suspicious. His embrace had felt more like a pat-down.

He unpacked his clothes and used the activity to look for video cameras or bugs. The obvious places, behind mirrors and tucked inside lamps, were clean. He looked under the table and checked for cracks in the walls where something might be hidden, but found nothing. The closet was also clean of any devices.

Pike crossed the room to the balcony. He pulled drapes aside, opened the sliding glass door, and let the saltwater-tinged air into the room. He overlooked the beach all right, the busy roadway in between him and the white sand. The blue water was very inviting, the beach covered with people jammed shoulder to shoulder, tanned and pale. The water was equally full, the rumble of the waves reaching him just fine despite the distance. He liked a day at the beach, but this was too much—no space to breathe.

He looked out at the hazy horizon, the water and sky a clear blue, and back toward land. Off to the left, a line of white buildings gave the appearance of being squeezed together to maximize the available space. Behind them were mountains with rolling peaks. No sign of Christ the Redeemer; Pike wondered if he would be struck down upon seeing the statue.

He knew what he was doing—plotting to murder a man—wasn't kosher. He'd never set out specifically to assassinate somebody. Any shooting he'd done had happened in self-defense or the defense of others. This time was different, though. He'd never been terribly religious or even spiritual, but deep down, he knew he was crossing a line.

But he would not turn away.

Pike took a deep breath. Back into the room. He dared not do anything to even suggested communicating with somebody on the outside, even Elsa. There would be no excuse for calling Elsa since she was technically on an assignment and shouldn't be disturbed under any circumstances. That meant not touching the cell phone currently burning a hole in his pocket. He decided to do exactly as Diego had suggested.

Picking up the telephone, he ordered bourbon and spring water from room service, along with a hot meal.

Pike lounged on the balcony, a drink in hand, staring at the sunset as the sun dipped into the ocean. He had a good buzz going. The time alone had revived him. When he heard the knock on the door, however, he jumped up with more vigor than he would have expected. Placing the drink on the dresser, he opened the door and found Diego and Elsa smiling at him.

"Reunited at last," Diego said.

Pike let both in and pecked Elsa on the cheek, catching a flash of jealousy in Diego's eyes.

"You two will want to get a good night's rest," Diego said. "We start early in the morning."

"You're happy with the tubes?" Elsa said.

"Delighted. Now we pick up the warheads and the detonators and put it all together."

"In Barcelona?" Pike said.

"No. Warheads here. Detonators in Barcelona." Diego smiled as Pike frowned. "What did I say about details, *mi amigo*? Follow my lead. I've been doing this a long time, right, Elsa?"

"As long as I've known you."

"See? Everything has been taken care of. All we need to do is be on time. With loaded guns—you know, in case things turn sour."

Diego smiled. Pike laughed. They all laughed.

"Forgive me, Marco. I'm used to fussing over details," Pike said.

Diego waved it off.

"Will you collect us or send a car?" Pike said.

"I'll be here, don't worry. I'll wait 'til after breakfast." He winked. "Good evening."

He left them alone.

Elsa placed her purse on the bed. "What do you think?"

Pike poured her some bourbon and water. "Quite a character."

"He's trying to figure you out." She took the offered drink and downed half of it.

"Figure what out?"

"Why you got me and he didn't. He tried every trick in his arsenal."

Pike edged closer to her. "So, why didn't they work?"

"I needed something more. Something real."

"Or maybe you like older guys?"

"Could be. They're certainly more experienced."

"That makes me sound ancient."

She set her drink down and moved closer, looking up into his eyes while reaching for his belt. "Do you feel old?"

"Not at all."

"Then put your drink down."

He did.

CHAPTER TWENTY-ONE

Diego wore a tan suit and a white shirt when he came to collect Pike and Elsa the next morning, but he did not object to their street clothes.

"I'm the one who will carry out the business," he said, "while you two stand guard. Let's see your hardware."

Pike had no problem showing Diego his gun, an old Browning Hi-Power he had carried for most of his career. Elsa had ditched her beloved mini-Uzi in the States and allowed Diego to inspect her backup gun, a compact pistol that had almost no sign of use on the frame. No scratches or scuff marks.

"You ever use this?" Diego said as he looked at the gun.

"Usually not," she said.

Diego approved of the weapons and led them downstairs to where the same sedan Pike had ridden in the day before waited. Different chauffeur this time, though.

The tinted windows again allowed only a partial view

of things, but Pike saw enough—the crowds of tourists, street vendors, busy shops, the beach once again stuffed to capacity. Buildings spit-shined and ready for updated pictures in the travel brochures. Clear blue sky and tall, rolling mountains with so much green one might think it was artificial. They followed the road out of the tourist area and into the deeper portions of Rio, where the buildings weren't as nice, the streets not as crowded, and the faces of the people were warier.

Still farther along Av. Rodrigues Alves, Pike looked out at cargo ships along the coast, each one either packed to capacity or almost, as goods were transferred to shore via huge cranes.

Traffic thinned out as they started through blocks of warehouses, the streets and sidewalks dusty with debris. The characters on the street corners didn't appear to be the welcoming type.

The driver slowed at a warehouse with boarded windows and a sign advertising it was available for lease. The sign was in three languages, including English. Single-level, it sat on the corner of Rodrigues Alves and Av. Prof. Pereira Reis. A beat-up Jeep was parked in the loading zone. The chauffeur pulled up across the street.

"Is this the place?" Pike said.

"I want you two to stay around the perimeter," Diego said. "I shouldn't be long."

"You're going in alone?" Elsa said.

"Of course, Elsa. My reputation demands it."

Diego exited first, followed by Pike and Elsa. The chauffeur kept the engine running.

They crossed the street, and Pike and Elsa separated to cover either side of the building. Diego tapped a code on a steel door, and when it opened, he slipped inside.

Elsa went over to Pike. "Shall we?"

Pike grinned.

She started around her side of the building. Pike followed the dusty concrete around his side. The boarded windows allowed not one inch of space to see inside. What was happening in there? He cared less for Diego's safety and more about the exchange. Diego hadn't brought cash. How was he paying? He reminded himself not to get too nosy. Too much sniffing might make him very dead.

Pike's shoes crunched on a patch of gravel. The wind picked up and tickled his neck. He rounded the back of the warehouse at the same time Elsa did. She smiled at him and smacked his rear end as he went by. He turned sharply, giving her a look, and she stifled a laugh. They kept going. Pike looked at their surroundings—more warehouses, equally empty, and what looked like a homeless camp about thirty yards away. Three tents, trash barrels clustered. No sign of bodies, though, living or otherwise.

As he rounded the front, Diego emerged from the door he'd entered, smiling, with two men behind him carrying a large case. Pike whistled for Elsa. The two men from the warehouse loaded the case into the trunk of the sedan. The rear end sank a little. Diego dismissed the two men,

and he, Pike, and Elsa climbed back inside. The driver
had them on the road within ten seconds. He drove a little
faster than the posted limit.

"Success?" Pike said, although he felt silly about it.
But Diego, still grinning, wasn't talking.

"Everything we need."

"Do we get to see it?"

"There's no reason for you to see it, *mi amigo.*"

"I'd like to know what I'm risking my life for," Pike
said.

"Good point. When we reach the hotel, I will show you
the warheads."

Elsa, in the front seat, looked back at Pike and smiled.

Diego lifted the trunk lid. The smaller trunk, nestled inside, was a dull gray. Diego snapped open the locks and
raised the lid.

"There they are," he said.

They were in the parking lot of the hotel, but nobody
passing by would pay any attention to what the trunk
contained, nor would they recognize the warheads for
what they were unless they were the proverbial rocket
scientists.

Cylindrical bullet-shaped objects about ten inches
long, made of bright stainless steel. Pike whistled. He lifted one from its protective foam and placed his left hand
near the nose. He felt the weight right away, the object

heavy, the surface so smooth he had no proper grip. He held on as long as he could before propping the tube upright in the foam. The middle section was hollow, and his throat dried up. That could mean only one thing: the warhead was built to have the explosive charge in front and the section for a chemical agent directly behind.

When placed in the tip of a missile such as could be built using the tubes he and Elsa had picked up in San Francisco, the warhead would detonate as soon as it struck the target. The explosion would accelerate the chemical agent into the atmosphere, spreading it over a wide area.

Pike unscrewed the front section and looked at the cavity where the explosive charge should be. There was no explosive or trigger.

"We still have some parts to collect," he said a little too coldly, placing the warhead back in the case.

"Indeed we do," Diego said. "That's what is waiting for us in Barcelona."

Diego slammed the trunk. He had to return to his safe house. He told Pike and Elsa to enjoy the rest of the day because they would be leaving in the morning.

"I know the perfect place to go," Elsa said, taking Pike's hand after Diego's sedan turned out of the parking lot.

"Where?"

"You like to dance, right?"

"Sure."

She squeezed his hand. "Trust me."

They went out for dinner and dancing. Pike put every ounce of energy into being present with Elsa, but in the back of his mind, he couldn't help but wonder where they'd get the chemical component for the missiles, and what type of chemical agent it would be. It wasn't like you could buy one on any corner.

His mission was becoming much more complicated than he'd anticipated.

CHAPTER TWENTY-TWO

Pike did not mind climbing back aboard the Gulfstream G550. Diego's private jet was outfitted with many luxury items, the best of which were probably the seats. The cabin, very cozy, was narrower because of the larger seats, which were upholstered in beige leather to match the carpet. Each chair reclined and rotated.

At the head of the cabin, near the cockpit, sat a dining table; toward the rear were the galley and restroom. Diego had no flight attendant, so whatever one needed, one had to fetch.

Every other seat shared a touchscreen mounted to the fuselage that could be adjusted via a metal bar to accommodate whoever wanted it. The large oval windows lining the fuselage let in plenty of light but tinted at the flick of a switch.

Diego and Pike stowed the luggage beneath the plane. A courier had arrived the night before to collect the missile tubes and the warheads to take to their next destination.

Diego had full confidence in the courier, but Pike had had questions, enough to make Diego laugh in exasperation. He once again promised Pike he had everything under control, but he did appreciate Pike's concern. He'd rather have a concerned colleague than one who didn't care about the mission.

He and Elsa sat near the front. Pike let his body sink into the leather seat, which was couch-comfortable. Despite the stress on his mind and body, he felt himself relax a little as the jet began to taxi.

"You were all by yourself on this plane last time?" Elsa said.

"Yup."

"Sorry I missed it," she said.

"I have a feeling only half of your regret applies to me."

Elsa laughed.

Diego sat near the back and began reading an exotic car magazine.

Elsa grabbed onto the armrests of her seat as the plane lurched into the sky.

"You okay?"

"Always get a bit nervous flying," she explained.

Pike reached out and touched a button below the oval window to Elsa's left. The tint took effect and shaded the outside view. He touched the sensor beneath his window too.

She smiled, her eyes showing her relief.

"Flying isn't for everybody," he said.

"I've never been able to get used to it."

Presently the jet leveled off.

"Want anything?" Pike said, removing his seatbelt.

"A gin and tonic."

"Coming right up."

Pike rose and dipped his head a little as he walked down the cabin. He didn't think he'd hit his head on the raised ceiling, but being careful wouldn't hurt. Slamming his head would.

"Drink run," he told Diego.

"I have a six-pack of beer on the bottom shelf," he said, not looking up from his magazine.

Pike busied himself in the galley, mixing the gin and tonic, grabbing Diego's beer, and fixing his own scotch and soda. The cramped galley had barely enough room for him to move around, and if he stopped to send a text on his phone, they might wonder about the delay and lack of noise. The restroom was probably going to be his best bet for privacy. He delivered the beer and Elsa's gin and tonic. She took a healthy sip and clutched the glass in both hands, her eyes nowhere near the window despite the tint.

Pike eased back into his chair. "Why don't you mess around on the computer?" He pushed the touchscreen her way. "We got everything on this plane, including high-speed wi-fi."

"What am I going to do with wi-fi?"

"Update Facebook?"

She laughed. Pike figured she needed something to keep her mind off flying. She had a nice laugh. It sounded like wind chimes in a gentle breeze.

Pike sipped his drink while Elsa played with the touchscreen, cursing at it now and then. He grinned. She didn't have any better luck with technology than he did, it seemed.

"Excuse me," he said after a while. She didn't notice. Whatever she had on the screen in front of her had done the trick. Pike went to the rear again. Diego had reclined his chair and was softly snoring.

Pike slipped into the restroom and locked the door. He leaned against the sink and let out a long breath.

He grabbed his cell phone from his jacket pocket. He had memorized the number of the burner phone. He typed in the number, selected the option to send a text, typed Is ANYBODY THERE? and hit SEND.

While he waited, he used the facility. Had to make it look good, after all. The phone vibrated twice as he was washing his hands.

Somebody *was* on the other end.

Somebody had received his message.

Who?

He dried them on a small towel and then looked at the responding note.

He was much calmer than he figured he'd be.

Stiletto and Nikki sat in a booth in the Hilton's restaurant. The cushion on Stiletto's side had a tear, with stuffing popping out. He pulled out some of the stuffing and played with it while Nikki sipped ice water. Neither had spoken since sitting down; in fact, they had been silent since their return from the DeSoto house.

After alerting General Ike to the developments in Marin, he ordered Stiletto to stand down while the technical crew at the Trust sorted through Oscar DeSoto's data at home and in his office. Scott expected an update soon.

Meanwhile, Stiletto had to distract himself, even for a moment, from the tension of trying to find John Pike's trail, and he had the perfect distraction in mind—if Nikki would cooperate. However, she might have to admit she wasn't perfect, and that was a tall order.

The tattooed waitress arrived with their food. Nikki started cutting her steak while Scott started on a burger dripping juice. He left the seat stuffing on the table.

"It's time to address the elephant in the room," Stiletto said.

"You've been building up the nerve to ask me, haven't you?"

"Why are you running?"

Her New York steak was slightly pink in the center. She chewed a piece as she looked off to the side.

"Hear about the discovery of new diamond deposits in Russia?"

"I don't waste time with the fake news media."

"There's a ton of the stuff waiting to be dug out of the ground there, right? Somebody managed to get some uncut stones out of the pits. I ripped that guy off, then somebody ripped me off. Then I stole them back, and the second guy has a crew out looking for me."

Stiletto laughed. "Don't bury the lede, Nikki. How did you lose them to begin with? Who in the world managed to rip *you* off?"

Nikki furiously cut into her steak. "Not telling."

Stiletto laughed again. "Must be a whopper. Did you turn your back at the wrong moment, or need to get laid so bad after the rip-off that you seduced the wrong guy and he stole the diamonds next?"

She stopped cutting and glared. She kept her head down but raised her eyes, and the fire behind them was tangible.

Stiletto's shoulders shook with laughter. "The second one. I *knew* it."

She raised the steak knife and said, "Not a word."

"You can't hurt me with that thing, Nikki."

"Open your mouth about this and I'll find something better."

Stiletto stopped laughing and ate some more of his burger. Nikki remained quiet.

"Your urges are going to get you in real trouble some-day," he said.

"You haven't complained when you've benefitted."

Stiletto's phone beeped, cutting off his snarky reply.

He took out his smartphone and read the screen.

"From my boss," Scott said. "The team went through what was left of DeSoto's files."

"What do you mean, 'what was left?'"

"They were all corrupted in one form or another. The woman spiked his files with a virus of some sort." Stiletto read more. "They did come up with a name on a contact list, James Fox. Mean anything to you?"

"Not off the top of my head."

"They're running a trace, so we'll know more soon."

Stiletto put down the phone and ate. The French fries were too salty.

The tattooed waitress stopped to ask Nikki if she wanted a refill on her coffee. She said no.

Stiletto frowned as something vibrated inside one of the other pockets of his jacket. It was the cell phone he'd found buried near Cupid's Bow. He put down the half-eaten burger and dug out the phone.

"Why do you have that antique?" Nikki said.

Stiletto lifted a finger. She paused. His eyes widened as he read the text message.

"I think it's Johnny," he said. "It says, 'Is anybody there?'"

Nikki didn't reply. Stiletto quickly punched in a reply. Sierra Two with Friend. He pressed the Send button a little too hard.

"We have to be careful," Scott said.

"Why?"

"Could be a trap, especially with what happened at DeSoto's."

"Don't be paranoid."

"Don't be unrealistic."

"Scott—"

He raised a hand as the phone vibrated again.

"'Stand by,'" Scott read.

"For what?"

"No idea."

Stiletto tapped his upper lip and started to reply when his phone beeped again too. He consulted his phone with a frown.

"Cops are looking for us," he said.

"What?"

"They saw a video of what happened in the garage. We got an APB out on us and everything. We're hot stuff."

Nikki pushed her plate away, the steak unfinished and already forgotten. "We leave. Now."

"Let's settle the bill and get out of here," Stiletto said.

CHAPTER TWENTY-THREE

Stiletto accelerated onto the freeway heading south for San José. There was a major airport there that would serve their purposes when the time to scoot arrived. Nikki sat in the passenger seat, her body tense, eyes forward.

"You okay?" he said.

"Somehow, knowing the cops *and* the killers are looking for my hide makes me a little nervous."

Stiletto nodded. The police APB could easily be intercepted by unfriendly parties, who would then know where to concentrate their search for Nikki Fortune. He might have to bail her out the same way she'd helped him.

The quiet purr of the motor filled the car. There was no sense in turning on the radio. Scott knew the only reason to do that was so they wouldn't have to talk, so silence was fine.

There wasn't much scenery to look at. Off to the left, where the bay was, a hint of city lights glowed on the other side of the bay. The black chasm between was the bay water, which might as well not have been there. To the right were the usual gas stations and roadside buildings, car repair shops, hotels, and a Porsche dealership. None of it was very exciting. Other cars sped by, their rear lights bright, but the cars were indistinguishable from one another.

His cell phone rang, breaking Stiletto's reflective spell.

He answered and said, "Don't you ever sleep, sir?"

The general laughed. "I'm up late just for you. Where are you?"

"Southbound on the 101 freeway," Stiletto said. "We thought it best to hit the road because of the APB."

"I have information. Are you ready?"

"I'll put you on speaker." He pressed a button and said, "Go."

The general's voice, very clear on the cell phone speaker, filled the cabin.

"First, let's start with the woman we saw in the pictures with John Pike. Her name is Elsa Suba, mid-thirties, a free-lance shooter for various terror cells. She's never appeared on our radar, but the Swiss and Germans want to talk to her about a couple of homicides. No known associates."

"You mentioned something about DeSoto's files earlier, General," Stiletto said. "A man named Fox. What about that?"

"I think that's our best lead. James Fox and DeSoto communicated a lot with each other."

"Who is he?"

"American expatriate with connections to the Russian mob," the general said. "Normally resides in Greece on an island not far from Crete, in a heavily-guarded home."

General Ike gave what the Trust had as a current location, but told him they had no eyes on Fox so the details could not be confirmed.

"We'll find him," Stiletto said.

"Fox is known to deal with anybody," the general said. "A few weeks ago, he sold a crate of missiles to Hezbollah. The following week, he made a deal with Israel for a supply of ammunition and explosives."

"Sounds like a real angel," Scott said.

"I'll have a local contact waiting for you, and he'll set up interrogation facilities," the general said.

Scott said, "We'll leave as soon as we can."

"Keep me updated."

Scott ended the call.

Nikki said, "Are you thinking what I'm thinking? I can't believe we're going to Greece."

"And Crete, no less."

The first time Stiletto had met Nikki and her father and enlisted their help to pursue a common enemy, they had raided a warehouse connected to said enemy that had also been on Crete, and it had been quite a battle. Enemy gunners had been waiting, and when Stiletto, Nikki, and their shipload of mercenaries arrived, the firing had started before one boot hit the jetty.

"Think it's the same place?" Nikki said. "Somebody bought the property we blew up and all that?"

Stiletto laughed. "Stranger things have happened."

Stiletto drove to San Jose International Airport, where they purchased plane tickets for the next flight to Greece, which left at 8:15 the following morning. After checking into a hotel near the airport, they both settled down for some much-needed rest.

On the plane, Stiletto fell asleep right away. He awoke after a while. Slivers of light crept through closed window shades and gave the cabin an eerie feel. He picked up one of the paperbacks Nikki had purchased prior to the flight, saw it was a noble vampire-werewolf billionaire shape-shifter step-sibling romance set in medieval times, set it down, and went back to sleep.

Nikki sat beside Stiletto with a Snickers in one hand and another book in the other.

They landed in Athens and collected their baggage. The contact arranged by General Ike was waiting near the baggage carousels, holding a white sign with the words Scott & Nikki scrawled in black marker. Stiletto identified himself, and they used the standard passcode of the week to confirm they both belonged to a silly fraternity of people who insisted on code phrases and put bugs in martini olives.

It kept the job interesting, at least—something to laugh

at. Stiletto needed to laugh to keep his mind from dwelling too much on the past.

The contact said he was Adrianos, a dark-skinned man with bushy eyebrows and a bushy mustache. He drove the agents away in a black Lincoln.

As he drove, Adrianos said, "Your hotel isn't far. We'll take off for Crete in the morning."

"Fine," Stiletto said. Nikki remained quiet.

"Too bad you're not here for fun. It's off-season, so you wouldn't have to fight the tourists."

"But we *will* fight somebody else," Stiletto said. "You can bet on that."

CHAPTER TWENTY-FOUR

Moscow was cold.

Sergei Vasilov of the Russian SVR, sipping coffee from an espresso cup, waited for the old man behind the desk to speak. His chief—about his age, his hair gone, his jowly face now a headquarters fixture—read from a report with glasses perched on the edge of his nose.

The office was as cold as the outside, with no personal touches. The boss did not like clutter. Everything on the desk was tidily arranged.

Vasilov welcomed the warm coffee as a sharp contrast to the outside chill. He didn't speak as his boss read. He had too much to hide. Anything he said before the boss reached the end of the report might expose what was on his mind, and what had really happened in Berlin.

Presently Ryndin Iosif, chief of the SVR, set down the papers and removed his glasses. His old eyes regarded Vasilov with little interest.

"A shame what happened in Berlin."

"Yes, sir."

"We lost two good men."

"We did."

"You were successful in eliminating Sallig Mahfi, but his chemical weapon remains on the loose."

"It does, sir."

"What do you suggest we do about that, Sergei?"

Vasilov drained the espresso and set the cup and saucer on the boss's desk. He sat back in his chair.

"We identified Morgan Lane as the buyer," he said. "She's in Vienna. I suggest we go see her. I'd like to go alone."

"Maybe it's best you work alone, considering your associates have a nasty habit of getting killed."

Vasilov only blinked in response. Iosif was trying to get a reaction out of him. Vasilov had lost men in the field before. Hazards of the job. But this was the first time he'd personally *shot* any of them.

"Do we want the chemical weapon or not, sir?"

Iosif said, "You will go to Vienna. The Kremlin wants this chemical agent out of circulation. Spare no expense."

"Is that all, sir?"

Iosif studied Vasilov's face, his puffy jowls suddenly standing out.

"You may go, Sergei. Shall I wish you good luck?"

Vasilov rose from the chair and buttoned his suit coat. "I may need it, sir."

Iosif only nodded.

Vasilov exited the office.

James Fox sipped from a coffee mug, the words on the side reading WORLD'S GREATEST ARMS DEALER.

Just one example of his odd sense of humor.

His office was well-lit and clean but without windows. He preferred not to have the distraction, especially on a nice day such as this, when the sky was clear and the ocean a perfect compliment.

The door opened, and one of his men entered. Fox examined Rufus Saye over the brim of his mug. Saye was one of his field officers. If he'd had a normal job, his title might be Sales Representative. His specialty was seeing deliveries through various obstacles to paying customers.

"Have a seat, Rufus," Fox said, setting the mug on the desk.

Saye sat and crossed his legs. He lit a cigarette. Fox turned on a desk fan to blow the smoke away.

"What's the job?" Saye said.

"We have several crates of automatic rifles that need to go to Africa," Fox said, handing Saye a thick manila folder from the clutter on the desk. The office was clean, but the desk was not, yet Fox never had trouble finding what he needed when it was required.

Saye paged through the file.

"Everything's been handled, but you'll have the usual slush fund for any surprises that come up," Fox said.

"Those guns belong to the man on the first page, nobody else. If anybody else tries to claim them, you have permission from the client to do what is necessary to get out of there."

Saye nodded and blew out a stream of smoke. The blast from the fan whipped the smoke in circles.

"Any questions?"

"It's routine, boss."

"Nothing is routine. Not right now."

"What do you mean?"

Fox shrugged. "This project with you-know-who is a little tense, that's all."

"Sure."

"Let me do the worrying, Rufus."

Saye jammed the cigarette in one corner of his mouth, nodded, and rose to leave. Fox watched his back as Saye shut the door. He left the fan running and looked around. It might be nice to have windows after all. Fox refilled his mug from the coffee maker on a shelf behind him and left the office to take in the view outside. He'd paid a lot for his private island; he might as well get some enjoyment out of it.

He climbed a narrow set of steps to the roof, the walls threatening to attack his elbows at any second. Emerging through the rooftop door, the fresh air and salt-scented breeze attacked him right away, and he squinted in the bright sunlight. The ocean roared, or whatever it was that oceans did when observed. He'd never tire of the chaos of the crashing waves.

He drank some coffee. He knew he shouldn't be concerned about Harrison Joule's plan to assemble a pair of chemical-warhead missiles, but in doing so, he was exposing them all to a great deal of risk. The risk might be worthwhile given the payoff and provide a nice cushion for all of them if they wanted to make a quiet exit, but Fox didn't like heat. Too much heat, and you ended up getting your neck snapped by the big killer Lagros.

He swallowed another mouthful of French roast and looked at the words on the mug. He knew that just finishing the job wouldn't save him. He'd have to take precautions if he wanted to keep breathing, and maybe sacrifice a few pawns. After the missiles sold, it would be time to get out and find somewhere to hide.

Maybe another private island. They were always for sale, especially when their owners died under suspicious circumstances, i.e., not killing themselves, which was known to happen. Now and then.

He had a capable crew at the present location. He spotted a few from the rooftop, carrying out their daily patrol of the territory surrounding his complex. The shores had landmines strategically placed to fend off any intruders and alert his men to their presence. He wouldn't be easy to capture. Or kill. He would take a bunch of them with him should circumstances point to no other resolution.

Stiletto cleared the breakfast dishes from the table so Adrianos could spread out a series of photographs.

"Latest satellite intel," The Greek's thick black mustache almost obliterated his mouth. "We'll approach from the eastern side. You can see Fox's home in this valley, hills on three sides, with the boat docks at the front. The seaplane anchored to the dock arrived a day ago."

"What kind of security are we facing?" Nikki said.

"Shore patrols, landmines, razor wire, and armed troops," Adrianos said.

"He doesn't mess around," Stiletto said.

"He's a man who must always watch his back. And his front. And both sides."

"Can we get SCUBA gear and slip in near the docks?" Stiletto said.

"The docks are the most heavily guarded. The eastern side is the best bet. Slip over the hill into the valley."

"If," Stiletto said, "we get through the landmines, the guards, and the razor wire."

Adrianos replied, "Should be a piece of cake."

"Easy for you to say," Nikki told him. "You get to stay on the boat."

"There are some benefits to my job, yes." Adrianos smiled.

The boat, blacked out and shaped like an arrow, what Adrianos called a "VSV-25," had a low, rakish profile, an enclosed cockpit, and twin engines that shoved the craft through the choppy Aegean waters. Destination: Kasos Island, a small patch of land with an even smaller population, where captains could find sea-savvy crewmen for their freighters, or those with money and a nefarious spirit could hire muscle.

They weren't going to Crete after all, but remembering how he and Nikki had first forged their relationship hadn't been bad. Scott had needed help at a time when he was on his own, with no backup or agency support. Nikki and her father had their own beef against the enemy Scott was pursuing, so they'd joined forces against a common enemy, and the connection remained strong. Scott couldn't say that about everybody in his life.

It did seem strange to count a Mafia princess and her father as friends. He chalked it up as another mystery of the spy business.

Adrianos sat at the controls. To Stiletto, the instruments looked like airplane gauges. He watched the boat's radar screen. Plenty of blips showed, but Adrianos paid no attention.

Stiletto and Nikki sat behind the stocky Greek, decked out in black fatigues and loaded with weapons and gear. Adrianos had supplied it all, including fresh ammunition for their personal pistols.

Nikki asked, "How much time?"

"Ten minutes," Adrianos said.

The fast-moving boat bounced a little. Adrianos corrected his course with a gentle turn of the wheel.

Stiletto looked at the radar screen and saw the outline of Kasos Island. Two smaller blips appeared near the shoreline. Adrianos cut back the throttle, threw another switch, and said, "They're patrolling in pairs. I turned on a static screen, so we'll look like a flock of birds or something."

"What happens if they open fire?" Stiletto said.

"Got a pair of missiles hidden in the roof. Heat-seekers."

"Only two?" Stiletto said.

"Only two," Adrianos confirmed.

The stocky Greek slowed the boat some more. The blips continued moving along Kasos' shoreline. Adrianos kept his eyes on the radar, one hand on the wheel, and the other hand on the throttle.

Stiletto sat and watched the Greek. Nikki shifted in her seat. She pulled one of her gloves off and started popping her knuckles.

"Don't," Stiletto said.

Nikki stopped. "I'm nervous."

"Nervous about being trapped on an island with me?"

"Nervous about you not being there if the worst happens."

He glanced at her. He wasn't used to her being that vulnerable. Nikki Fortune was a tough nut for anybody to crack, but here she was, letting him into her state of mind. Knowing she had assassins on her trail must have influenced the statement. She didn't return Scott's look. She stared straight ahead and behaved as if she'd said nothing.

Adrianos throttled forward as the radar showed the patrols reaching the opposite side of the island. They neared the shore.

CHAPTER TWENTY-FIVE

Stiletto and Nikki raced up the beach. The hard-packed sand made it easy to run. They had the weather on their side. The bright, full moon, covered by clouds, provided no light for any troops who were nearby. With their black fatigues, they melted into the shadows.

From the beach, they started up the rocky slope. Stiletto's legs screamed as he kept up long strides. Nikki, almost without any effort, stayed a little ahead of him, her boots digging hard into the hill with each step. She gripped a handheld computer, glancing at the LCD display as they climbed. When she held up her left hand, they stopped and dropped flat.

"Land mines five yards ahead," she said, showing Stiletto the LCD display on which blue dots indicated the mines. Satellites above scanned the beach and fed the information to the computer in real-time.

Stiletto scanned the area with a pair of night-vision goggles.

"No troops," he said. "They must expect the mines to do most of the work this far out."

Nikki flipped a switch on the black box. "Mines are spaced enough apart for us to slip through if we stay single-file."

"Not very encouraging."

"Follow me," she said, rising. Stiletto pushed to his feet and dropped in line behind her. The nervousness she'd admitted to on the boat seemed to have vanished. She had a task to focus on now, instead of waiting for action. Sometimes that was all one needed to get out of a funk.

Twenty-five yards later, after marking the "safe zone" they'd walked through, Stiletto and Nikki dropped flat again, side by side.

Stiletto lay on a rock that poked through his fatigue shirt and into his stomach. He raised himself a bit and brushed the rock away. He made another scan with the night-vision goggles. "Still no troops."

Nikki started forward, then stopped; Stiletto froze, too. The whipping rotor blades of a helicopter increased in volume. From their left, the chopper, running lights flashing bright, flew into view. Stiletto and Nikki remained still. The chopper curved left, heading for the valley below.

"Party tonight?" Nikki said.

"Could be a regular patrol."

"What do you think?"

"Split up and see what we can find."

"See ya." Nikki created a small rockslide as she bolted from their position.

Stiletto watched her fade into the shadows. He didn't want to see her get hurt, and his immediate instinct was to follow and cover her, but his job wasn't to be her shepherd. In spite of her fears, Stiletto knew there was nothing she couldn't handle.

He went right, the angle of the slope making it hard to move quickly, angling toward the top of the hill so he could look into the valley at Fox's spread.

He stayed flat and rolled over the top, sliding down the slope. On this side there was more cover, some vegetation and small trees. He crawled to a tree trunk and examined the property through the goggles. The house was huge and at least two stories, with a circular turret and a clock tower-like structure rising from the center of the roof. A smattering of armed troops moved about. He saw the chopper on a landing pad, a crew going over the engine while the pilot scribbled notes on a clipboard. He zoomed in on the house. Some lights burned inside, and he wondered which room Fox was in. Judging by the number of troops, he and Nikki were Chihuahuas who had picked a fight with a lion. The smart move was to pull back and organize a full strike team.

He toggled his earpiece. "Sierra Two calling Trainwreck."

The call sign had been Nikki's idea.

Silence in his ear.

Stiletto swallowed and looked left, scanning the foliage for any sign of movement. Either Nikki couldn't answer, or for some reason, wouldn't. He tried again.

"Trainwreck, come back."

Stiletto's heart rate increased as he scanned the property. None of the troops behaved as if they were on alert for intruders. He watched a cluster of men light cigarettes, sharing the same lighter.

He let out a breath and carefully rose, staying low as he moved in the direction Nikki might have gone. The slope of the hill made it hard to stay upright. He slipped and fell hard on his left shoulder, stifling a grunt, then froze as a rifle cocked behind him.

"Do not move."

Stiletto felt the point of the rifle's barrel dig into his back.

"Put your weapon on the ground."

The trooper spoke without any hint of an accent. American?

Stiletto complied, setting his assault rifle aside.

"Hands up."

Stiletto lifted his hands, fingers splayed.

"On your feet."

Stiletto put a foot under him and rose, shifting to keep his balance.

"Turn."

Stiletto rotated and faced the trooper. He was young and fit, with a prominent chin. Other shadows closed in, more men with rifles, as young as the first, one with a radio who said they were bringing in one intruder. Stiletto noted they didn't mention a second.

CHAPTER TWENTY-SIX

Nikki heard Stiletto on the radio, but she was too close to danger to respond.

She watched four troops pass around a lighter and torch their cigarettes. She was flat on her belly in the foliage and waiting for them to move. Once the way was clear, she saw a path straight to the house and an unguarded side door.

When Stiletto went silent, she figured he was on the move, coming her way.

The chill of the night tickled her neck, but she ignored the urge to pull up her collar. The troops puffed smoke and started sharing dirty jokes. Typical. They wore weapons over their shoulders, not in a ready position; these guys weren't used to hard work. With a rifle and scope, she could take them all out at long distance before anybody realized they were under fire.

Then somebody's radio squawked. The jokes stopped, and they tossed their smokes, grabbed their weapons, and ran off. Other troopers, suddenly on alert, maintained positions near the house. It wasn't long before she saw what caused the alert: three troops, with Scott in front of them, hands high, cleared the foliage and marched across the property toward the house.

Nikki flicked the selector switch on her rifle to single shot. She could take a few out and let Stiletto get away, then they could head for the beach and the fancy boat with the missiles.

Here goes nothing.

She tucked the stock into her shoulder and—

"Stop."

A gruff voice behind her.

"Step away from the weapon."

Nikki dropped her assault rifle and rose to her knees, hands out, turning to look at the trooper. He was a kid. An American, by the sound of his voice. Had Fox poached discharged US troopers? The kid blinked when he saw Nikki's face in the light from the house.

"What's the matter, kid?" she said. "Never seen a woman before?"

James Fox walked down the white-walled hallway, wondering if he was the recipient of good fortune or if the captured intruders meant the fun was over and Joule's plot had been foiled.

The leader of his protective force had personally alerted him to the capture of the American intruders. He'd ordered the pair locked in his private dungeon. They were the first individuals ever to be so treated. When he'd built the complex, he decided he'd wanted a dungeon just because. He'd filled the walls with various torture devices from days gone by because it amused him. He wanted to tell people, "I have a dungeon." It made him seem dangerous. But with tongue planted firmly in cheek, he wondered if anybody ever believed he'd make use of the room. Well, today, he would. It probably already had a softening effect on his captives; they'd surely tell him everything he wanted to know about the level of interest in his activities.

Fox stopped at a doorway where a soldier stood guard. The trooper opened the door for Fox, who began his descent into the darkened room. He felt a chill up his neck. Heck, the dungeon was giving him the creeps; he could only imagine how the captured Americans felt.

Time to find out.

"I hope you have a plan to get out of here," Nikki said.

"When we don't check in with Adrianos, he'll send in the cavalry. Sit tight."

"My arms, legs, even my rear end, are numb."

"Then you're going to have a hard time."

"You're no help, Scott."

He smiled.

The troops had escorted the two of them into the basement of the house, a room with bare walls and nothing to suggest they ever expected any kind of company. The troops had tied their hands behind their backs and their ankles together and left them propped against the wall. The door was at the top of a narrow set of steps with no rail, and Nikki supposed they were fortunate not to have been shoved to the floor. The concrete floor was cold to the touch. A bare lightbulb in the ceiling dimly lit the room; most of the walls were shrouded in shadow.

"I've been in worse places," Stiletto said.

"Where?"

"Disneyland."

She frowned. A beat of silence stretched between them.

"Come on, that's funny."

"I know it is," she said, "but my funny bone is numb, too."

She swallowed. Her dry throat signaled more than thirst. Nobody was coming to rescue them. They were totally on their own.

"What are you thinking, Scott?"

"I'm wondering what's on these walls."

"That's not helping, either."

"What are *you* thinking?"

She paused before answering. "I'd rather not say."

The door swung open, and a shaft of light filled the room.

"I had to come and meet my guests," the new arrival announced, stomping down the steps. The shaft of light lit the arrival. Male. Tall. Blond hair. Jeans and a dark sweater. Combat boots. "My name is James Fox. I own this place. Why have you intruded on my property?"

Stiletto and Nikki said nothing.

"Are you deaf? Do I need to speak louder?" Fox wandered over to the far wall and took a whip from its place. He uncoiled it and snapped it once. The sharp crack filled the room, piercing Nikki's ears. She flinched.

"I thought that would get your attention." He approached and stopped a few feet from them. Looking at Nikki, he said, "So start talking, or I mark up the lady's face."

"She's the boss," Stiletto said. "I'm here to look pretty."

"You *ass*."

Fox laughed. "She better start talking," he said, shifting to Stiletto, "or *you* get the whip."

"Shut up and do it already," Nikki said. "This guy's been annoying me with stupid jokes ever since you locked us down here."

"And she's annoying me," Stiletto added, "simply by existing."

"Know what I'm thinking *now*, Scotty? Fox, untie me and give *me* the whip. I'll torture him myself."

"I may let you," Fox said.

Fox raised his right arm and brought the whip down with a sickening crack. Stiletto yelled. The point of the whip ripped open the front of his shirt, drawing blood.

"The tip is barbed, by the way," Fox said.

Stiletto groaned, dropping his head.

"Why are you here?" Fox said. "Who sent you? We have all night. I mostly sleep during the day."

Stiletto sagged forward, groaning again.

"Would you like a taste, my dear?" He took one step toward Nikki.

Fox raised his arm.

CHAPTER TWENTY-SEVEN

Stiletto pulled his bound legs close to his body, rising to his knees as Fox raised the whip above his head. Stiletto's right hand flashed in an arc, the overhead bulb glinting on a sliver of steel between his fingers. He made contact with Fox's right leg, slashing, tearing fabric, and drawing blood. Fox screamed, staggering back. Stiletto lunged clumsily and slashed a second time. Fox fell back, landing hard, the breath leaving his body. Scott pulled himself forward with his hands, pushed up on his left, and punched Fox as hard as he could.

Stiletto rolled onto his back, sat up, and used the sliver of metal on the ropes holding his ankles together.

"What the hell is that?" Nikki said.

"Razorblade hidden in my belt. Old trick."

The ropes fell free, and Stiletto crawled over to Nikki. He slashed her ankle ropes and then freed her arms.

"Shake it off, like Taylor says," he told her, supporting himself on the wall while he stood. "We gotta move."

"Are we taking him?"

"You bet."

"Weapons?"

"We'll have plenty of weapons, don't worry."

Stiletto hoisted Fox over his shoulder in a fireman's carry. Nikki grabbed the whip. They moved up the stairs as fast as they could, Stiletto straining under the other man's weight. Through the door and into a bright hallway—

A lone trooper waited there. He grabbed for a holstered handgun, and Nikki swung the whip. The lash wrapped around the trooper's wrist and she pulled him toward her, then pivoted, flashing her right leg out to backspin-kick the trooper in the chin. His head snapped back. She let go of the whip as he fell.

"Nice," Stiletto said.

"Old trick," she said, grabbing the trooper's pistol and the rifle he'd set against the wall. She gathered up his spare ammo belt and tightened it around her waist.

Stiletto shifted Fox's weight. "Gotta move."

Nikki led the way, with the rifle at her shoulder.

They wouldn't have an easy time getting out, but with the boss over his shoulder, Stiletto knew the troops wouldn't risk hurting him. He and Nikki moved down the hall to another staircase. The door above looked vacant, with no light spilling underneath the crack. Nikki went up first and opened the door, then motioned Stiletto forward. Breathing hard, Scott took the steps slowly. He didn't know how much Fox weighed, but it was more than Scott would have guessed.

They stepped into a furnished room with lots of wood on the floor and walls, dark leather chairs a match, and a curtained window across the way. Nikki made for the window and pulled the curtains back. Scott stopped behind her. Outside, the property appeared quiet. The chopper sat on its pad with nobody in attendance.

"Can you fly that thing?" he asked.

"You mean, you can't?"

"Nope."

"What do we do?" Nikki said.

"Run for the beach, then."

Nikki moved left, Stiletto following, down another short hallway. She stopped, turned, and started the opposite way. "Side door I saw earlier," she said. Stiletto hustled to keep up, shifting the weight on his shoulders again. He didn't know how much longer he could carry their quarry.

Stiletto and Nikki slipped out the side door and the cold night wind greeted them, as well as a cluster of troops who had been smoking earlier. They were still smoking and talking, and when one saw Nikki, he shouted an alarm.

Nikki's rifle spoke, a short string of rounds crackling. The trooper who'd shouted jerked and fell against one of his buddies, the others raising their weapons. Then somebody noticed Fox. They kept their weapons pointed at Stiletto and Nikki but did not fire.

"Stay back," Nikki said. As she and Stiletto started for the edge of the foliage, another trooper shouted into the radio. Nikki triggered another burst that kicked up dirt at their feet, and the troops scattered for cover. Somebody took a shot, which whistled over Scott's head. He moved a little faster, starting up the slope, Nikki pounding behind him. The foliage bit at Scott's ankles as he ran, the weight on his shoulders slowing him down, a hot flush crawling up his neck.

"Faster, Scott!"

Stiletto grunted in reply. The top of the slope was visible but seemingly ten miles away. The pursuit force was assembling behind them, men shouting, scattered shots coming their way but striking nowhere close. Nikki pulled ahead, stopping and turning to cover Stiletto as he struggled upward. She fired single shots at random, the flash from the muzzle highlighting the concentration in her eyes.

Stiletto pulled past her and over the slope. "Move!"

Flashes of automatic weapons fire lit the valley below. Stiletto had figured wrong. The troops weren't terribly concerned about hitting the boss.

Shots from behind kicked up dirt around him. Nikki fired a full-auto burst, cutting down two pursuing troops and driving the others back to cover. Scott ran past her and she jumped to her feet, following. He dropped to one knee a few yards up the slope, gasping.

"Scott!"

"Give me a second."

"We don't have a second!" She fired again, the rifle clicking empty. She slapped a new magazine and chambered a round. "Come on!"

She continued a few more yards, then turned back and fired another full-auto string as Stiletto edged past and gained more ground.

They continue the leapfrog-and-fire movement, keeping the troops back until they reached the beach, Scott still huffing and puffing. Nikki yelled as they neared the minefield and the safe zone they'd marked. Stiletto and Nikki hustled through the path and cleared the mines as troops reached the top of the hill behind them. Bullets zipped overhead and kicked up sand. Scott set Fox down. Nikki aimed at the hillside, scanning for targets. None so far.

The black arrow-like VSV-25 lay close to shore. Twin spotlights burned from the nose, lighting the hill, as troops crested the rise. The light drove them back to cover. Stiletto and Nikki splashed through the water. She held the hatch for Scott, who dropped Fox inside and climbed in after him. Nikki followed and pulled the hatch closed.

Adrianos killed the spotlights and swung the boat around, shoving the throttle forward. The engines roared, and the boat lurched. Nikki fell into her seat, and Stiletto braced himself on the hull as he took off his belt and wrapped it tight around Fox's wrists after pulling the man's arms behind his back.

The stink of saltwater and burned gunpowder filled the cabin.

"Strap in," the stocky Greek said. "Those patrol boats are behind us!"

The VSV-25 cut left and away from the oncoming patrol boats, which opened up with heavy machine guns. The slugs sliced through the waves and nicked the back and side of the VSV. A section of the enclosed roof slid open, and a pod with two missiles rose. The rockets fired, white contrails following the streaking missiles. Each struck a patrol boat dead center, and the explosions lit the night.

Before the flash of flame had faded, the seaplane zoomed around the wreckage, skimming the surface of the water. The wing-mounted machine guns blazed and strafed across the deck of the VSV. The boat cut right as the seaplane swooped overhead.

In the boat, Stiletto and Nikki strained against the seat restraints as Adrianos executed the evasive maneuvers. Stiletto said, "You should upgrade the missile system!"

"Funny, the intel didn't say the plane had guns!"

"There's always something they miss!"

Stiletto snatched Nikki's rifle. "Open the hatch!"

"Are you crazy?" she said.

Adrianos hit a switch, and the roof hatch opened. Stiletto extended his body through it, his shoulders clearing the opening. The harsh wind and stinging sea-spray struck his face and neck. He wiped blinding water from his eyes as the seaplane finished its turn and fired again. Stiletto squeezed off a burst. The plane angled sharply, making a wide turn. Stiletto fired at the plane's belly. The plane turned back, coming at the boat head-on. Adrianos hit the front spotlights. The plane wavered but kept coming. Stiletto fired a long burst, and the rifle clicked empty. The plane zoomed overhead. Stiletto handed the empty carbine to Nikki, who gave him her fully-loaded weapon. The seaplane approached again from the back, and the wing guns flashed. Rounds hit the water, smacked the hull, and whistled over Stiletto's head.

Stiletto held back return fire and let the plane get closer, then aimed for the cockpit and squeezed the trigger. The pilot turned, and Stiletto's rounds strafed the right side, shattering the windows.

The plane straightened and began to turn back again. Stiletto cursed. He bent back into the boat. "I missed."

"Try this!" Nikki broke open the emergency kit, hauled out a wide-barreled gun and a flare, and loaded the gun.

She handed it to Scott, who went through the hatch again.

The seaplane fired, coming at the VSV from the port side, more slugs tearing into the hull. Stiletto held his fire. The machine guns went silent as the plane turned to repeat the pass, and when it did, Stiletto fired the flare gun.

The bright flare smashed through the shot-out passenger side window. Bright light burned inside the plane and the wings dipped from side to side, then the plane straightened and dipped left. The nose followed the rest of the plane, and it crashed onto the surface of the ocean, then exploded. The heat of the blast singed Stiletto's face as he slipped back into the boat. He pulled the hatch closed.

Stiletto wiped his wet face and hair and plopped hard into the seat next to Nikki. His shoulders slumped; he breathed heavily.

"Good shooting," she said.

"Cool idea," he told her.

The stocky Greek said, "We're clear!"

"Can we go home now?" Stiletto asked.

Adrianos let out a laugh and steered for Crete. Stiletto and Nikki looked at each other.

"Still nervous?"

She grinned. She moved a hand up his left leg to his crotch. "More like the other thing now."

He slapped her hand. She pulled back with a shocked expression.

"Down, girl."

She balled a fist, but Stiletto grabbed her arm. She snapped, "You little—"

"Not in front of the driver, dear."

Adrianos laughed. Nikki relaxed and slumped in the chair with folded arms.

CHAPTER TWENTY-EIGHT

They smelled him right away. Fox hadn't bathed since his delivery to the basement of a building in Athens owned by the Trust. The basement came complete with holding/interrogation cells for situations such as the one in which Scott and Nikki found themselves. They'd let Fox sit for two days while they dug into his background and "recuperated" from the island adventure.

Guards had let Fox use a restroom after every meal, but that was the extent of his luxuries. Fox raised his head and looked with tired eyes at the new arrivals.

Stiletto and Nikki sat on folding chairs they'd brought, looking down at the prisoner. Scott rested a briefcase on his lap and popped the locks. "It's not very nice here, is it?"

Fox looked at a chip in the concrete floor.

Stiletto said, "You're waiting for us to torture you, right?"

Fox's nostrils flared, his breathing still labored.

"What will happen when we're done, whether you talk or not, is that you will face charges for selling weapons, and I do not doubt that you will spend the remainder of your life in prison."

Fox glared.

"We're fully capable of keeping you here for the rest of your life, Fox. Who says you need to see the inside of a courtroom? That's your future. You can remain silent or give us what we want. There's no reason to drag your mother into this."

At the mention of the word "mother," Fox's eyes snapped to Stiletto's face. The rest of his expression did not change.

Scott took out a photo from the briefcase and placed it on the floor between her and Fox.

"She looks like a classy lady. Probably deserves a better son than you. If you refuse to tell us what we want to know, I will send my partner," Scott gestured to Nikki, "to kill her."

Fox's neck flushed red.

"I know what's going through your mind," Stiletto continued, "she's a schoolteacher and never committed a crime in her life. I'm sure she's taken paperclips home from work, and that makes her a criminal, so I won't lose any sleep, and neither will my friend here if we shoot bullets into her."

Fox said, "You wouldn't."

"I most certainly would," Stiletto said. From another

pocket of the briefcase, he retrieved a stack of pictures wrapped in a rubber band. He removed the rubber band and began setting out the pictures as if he were dealing a hand of poker. Each picture showed Fox's mother at various points of a day: arriving at and departing from work, loading groceries into her car, at a restaurant with friends. A time stamp on each picture indicated they had been snapped over the last forty-eight hours.

Fox began breathing a little faster.

"Tell me a story, Fox." Stiletto focused his eyes on Fox's.

"You can't hurt her," the man said.

"We won't if you cooperate."

"May I have a sip of water?"

Stiletto nodded to Nikki; presently, she returned with a glass. She held the glass for Fox and let him take a drink.

"There's this group," Fox said, "led by a man named Harrison Joule. They want to build two chemical missiles and sell them to the highest bidder."

"Not use the missiles themselves?" Stiletto said.

Fox shook his head. "Joule brokers deals like this. He's getting too old to work in the field, so he buys or builds weapons and lets somebody else use them."

"Who is he?"

"Joule has been with the radical underground for decades. He'll be in your records. I only see him once or twice a year when we have our meetings. Mostly, I deal with a woman named Elsa Suba. She represents him in the field."

"Does the name Oscar DeSoto mean anything to you?"

"DeSoto designed the missile tubes. The warheads are coming from another source."

"The missile parts are being collected?"

"That's in progress."

"They haven't been assembled?"

Fox shook his head.

"Where is Elsa Suba?"

"I don't know. But I know who might."

"Who?"

"Another woman. She is selling the chemical weapon we're putting into the missiles. Her name is Morgan Lane."

Stiletto showed no reaction, but his mind went into overdrive. *Chemical weapon?* A standard missile was bad enough in the wrong hands, but a chemical attack on any major city in the world would be catastrophic.

He'd witnessed enough chemical weapons attacks to know how deadly they could be.

"Don't go anywhere," Stiletto said with half a smile before leaving the room. Nikki remained.

Stiletto's update with General Ike was brief. Because of the time difference, his call had awoken the general, but his boss listened without comment until Scott had finished.

"Are you sure about all this?"

"No doubt, General."

Stiletto stood in another part of the basement, talking on his cell. He leaned against the wall opposite the interrogation room. Through the small window in the door, he could see the back of Nikki's head as she kept an eye on Fox.

The general said, "That at least moves us forward."

"We might know where to go next regarding this Morgan Lane person I've never heard of, but why didn't we know a chemical weapon was on the market?"

"Probably because it wasn't."

"What do you mean?"

"It might be leftover inventory from the Soviets, as we've dealt with before, or somebody created it, which isn't outside the realm of possibility, or they somehow acquired the weapon on the black market and we missed the information. *Where* they got it isn't the question. How we stop them *is*."

"Yes, sir."

"What are your plans now?"

"We'll do some digging on Lane," Scott said. "If we're facing somebody who has the infrastructure to house and sell a chemical weapon, I'm going to need a backup unit."

"I will see who is available and send them your way."

Stiletto and his boss ended their call as Nikki exited the interrogation room. She said the room was getting stuffy.

Adrianos tapped his keyboard. He sat behind his desk in a dimly lighted office, Stiletto and Nikki standing behind him.

"Here we go," the Greek said as a picture and dossier appeared on the screen. "Morgan Lane. We don't have much on her. Got her start running with German anarchists when she was in college."

"She's exactly your type, Scott," Nikki said.

"Now, now," Stiletto said.

"Are we done playing around?" Adrianos said.

Stiletto said, "Can we run a coordinate check on the location Fox provided? I want to make sure he's not sending us on a wild goose chase."

Adrianos consulted the interrogation notes and tapped more keys.

CHAPTER TWENTY-NINE

Harrison Joule, within the warm confines of his hilltop cabin, spoke into a burner cell phone. "Where are you, Marco?"

"On our way to meet with Ferguson and collect the detonators."

"Any trouble on your end?"

"None. Yet."

"Remain on alert."

"All right. What else is there?"

"We lost Fox."

"How did that happen?"

"I don't know. There was a raid on his island, and he vanished, so we must assume he's in a hole somewhere."

"The IRA?"

"I don't think so. Better not be. Not after we worked out our differences."

"Who, then?" Diego said.

"I'm at the cabin. I'm about to meet with the others

and ask them nicely if anybody has talked. Somehow, word of our operation may have leaked."

"Perhaps somebody talked about the invitations?"

"The invites said nothing about what offered, only that I have something for sale," Joule countered.

"And whoever did this would have to know of your affiliation with Fox."

"Might have come from DeSoto. We have as many unanswered questions with DeSoto as we do with Fox."

Harrison Joule stopped talking for a moment as he turned over a new thought in his mind.

"Are you there?" Diego said.

"Marco, have the new man or Elsa done anything suspicious?"

"Neither have been out of my sight long enough to talk to anybody they shouldn't be talking to."

"What about when they're alone?"

"Elsa is a loyal member of our cause, Harrison. Even if John Pike wanted to tell somebody, how could he? He's in the same bed as her."

"There is a leak somewhere. There might be only one way to fix this."

"What are you thinking?"

"We have to sweep the house clean and start over, Marco."

"I hope that doesn't mean—"

"Of course not. Good luck with Ferguson, and don't let anybody stop you."

Harrison Joule ended the call.

He sat at the long table in the cabin's center, looking at the empty seats.

The clock was ticking, and there wasn't time to spend wondering who had let the secret slip.

He had to make sure nothing ruined the operation and put him at the end of a gun or in prison. They all had to die.

Joule stood outside the door of the log cabin with a cup of steaming English Breakfast in one hand. He watched the line of vehicles approach the building, a sight he'd seen many times, but tonight would be the last time with this crew. He felt a little bad. He'd grown to like his associates, his backers, his supporters, but somebody had talked. He'd build another crew.

He would miss his garden, but gardens could be planted anywhere. He'd plant another and enjoy that too.

Three Land Rovers, headlamps bright, pulled up to the cabin. Three men stepped out. Harrison Joule sighed. Only three left.

The Eastern European, Pavic. The Brits, Gambelin and Tunison.

DeSoto was gone. Fox was gone.

DeSoto might have been a planned liquidation, but Fox had not.

"What's happening?" Pavic said, cutting in front of the Brits as the three men approached the cabin. "You said it was an emergency."

"Inside," Joule ordered.

The four men entered. Joule pulled the door closed. The door blocked the night's chill with quiet finality.

As his men sat, Joule looked at their faces. None of them seemed nervous. They were curious.

Joule hooked his hands behind his back and began a slow circle of the table. He slid a hand into his right jacket pocket and wrapped his fingers around the wooden grip of an S&W Model 19 .357 revolver.

"What's the meaning of this, Harrison?" said Tunison.

Joule froze and stared down the stocky Brit. When Joule worked for Jimmy Reardon and the IRA, he would have shot Tunison simply for existing.

Some things never changed.

"We have a problem," Joule began. "There is a leak. DeSoto is dead. Fox is missing. Somebody has said something to somebody they shouldn't have, and now we need to decide what to do about it. Gentleman, have any of you spoken of our activities? Even by accident? Anything about what we're doing?"

The three men exchanged looks, confused one they then transferred to Joule.

Harrison Joule straightened a little. Was he wrong about his crew? Or was somebody a better liar than Vracek had ever been?

He continued. He explained the situation further—the threats to their current project, his conversations with Jimmy Reardon and the IRA, with Marco Diego. Everything.

He told them he was positive the IRA wasn't involved. Somehow, Western Intelligence had learned of their operation, and that meant loose ends had to be tied up. And while it pained him, there was only one way to settle matters.

Pavic was the first to stand and object loudly, and Joule shot him through the right eye.

Gambelin fell back in his chair and hit the ground hard as Joule fired. The bullet zipped over the Brit's head.

Tunison wasn't so lucky. He lifted his chair to swing at Joule, but he dodged to one side, fired twice, and put two .357 slugs through Tunison's chest.

Gambelin crawled frantically for the front door.

Joule raised his gun and fired the remaining rounds in the cylinder, each hollow-point slug punching through the man's back. There was enough space between the body and the door for Joule to leave, and as he lowered the Smith & Wesson, he took one last look around the interior of his beloved cabin.

He departed in one of the Land Rovers, heading down the access road.

Halfway along, an orange flame filled his rearview mirror as the explosives he'd placed around the cabin foundation detonated. The fire would consume the cabin, the bodies, and his garden. He *would* miss the garden.

Harrison Joule looked forward and continued to drive.

Only the mission mattered now. Once he sold the missiles with their chemical warhead payload, he could buy all the cabins he wanted and put a garden in the back of each one.

"We land soon," Diego said. He joined John Pike and Elsa Suba at the table near the front of the jet's cabin, where he'd been on the phone for a long time.

As he sat, he produced some notes from the inside pocket of his jacket. Pike frowned. All their hopping about left him tired and sore, never mind the mental strain of keeping his cover, and the added strain of knowing his old pal Scott Stiletto was trying to track him down. He was beginning to seriously doubt his choices in this matter, but those choices couldn't be reversed. He had to finish. When he finished, if he survived, he'd face the consequences.

The CIA had fired Stiletto for going rogue. He more than likely would face the same fate, but with the added risk of losing his pension and benefits.

But what good were those things when his wife's killer still roamed free?

"Our job now," Diego said, "is to collect the detonators the missiles require. Without them, they won't explode on impact, and if they don't, our clients will be a little upset.

"But we have a problem. The boss discovered somebody in the organization betrayed us to a group of IRA gunners who want the detonators for their own project. We might have to deal with them up close and personal if you know what I mean. John, you and your Browning might get quite a workout."

"How long have you known about this?" Pike said. He didn't like the news. It was a complication. If either of them or, heaven forbid, *he* was taken out by the IRA crew, the whole mission was for naught.

"A few days. The boss has already dealt with the traitor in-house, and he tried to deal with the IRA men, but they slipped through the net. We have to assume they'll have tracked us, somehow."

"Can we get some more guys?"

Diego chuckled. "We're all there is, *mi amigo*. It's a small operation."

"You're telling me this boss of yours can't find more men to make sure his detonators get where he wants them?"

"That's why we hired you," Diego said. "You're the extra hand."

"They won't back down," Pike said. "I know the IRA. They'll show up. They'll buzz around like flies over a corpse."

"You'll have to be ready for them. Make sure none of us becomes this corpse."

"Don't worry," Pike said.

"You have an axe to grind with the Irish?"

"A big one," Pike said. "The IRA killed my wife in Belfast back in the '70s when we were there on another job."

Elsa made a sympathetic sound, and Diego's eyes never left Pike's face.

It was a tactical admission. There was no harm in it. The statement was far enough from the truth that Pike could take advantage of any question that might come up.

"I would hate to deprive you of your late revenge, *mi amigo*," Diego said. "I hope you can handle them."

"We'll see," Pike said. "I still think it's silly not to call for back-up."

Diego nodded. "I know. But what can I do? I'm following orders. I don't make decisions."

"What happens after we get the detonators? There's still a piece missing."

Diego smiled.

"The missile payload is our last stop before we take a well-deserved rest."

Kevin O'Rourke and Sean Collins sat at the bar, making small talk and taking turns watching the entrance via the big mirror behind the bar.

O'Rourke had not been much for talking in the days since Sally's murder in Belfast. He harbored cold anger toward Joule and his people, and he was going to even the score, if only a little, tonight. Once he had delivered the detonators to the army council, he'd target Harrison Joule, orders or no orders.

The third member of their team, Timmy Blaine, sat

alone on the other side of the bar, alternating his attention from the piano player in a corner to his partners to the front entrance.

"The couple that walked in could be them," O'Rourke said.

"The woman's wearing a scarf," said Collins. "She's not expecting a fight."

"But she hasn't removed her coat."

"Neither have you, Kevin. It's a wee bit chilly in here."

O'Rourke drank down his Scotch. The bartender wandered over and asked if he wanted a refill, but O'Rourke waved him off. He spotted a lone man carrying a case enter the restaurant and look around. The hostess approached him, but he said something to her and moved toward a table not too far from the couple.

O'Rourke said, "There's Ferguson."

"Sitting alone," said Collins.

"There's Diego."

"Nice of him to be on time."

"Finish your drink, Sean."

Diego pulled a chair over from another table and sat with the man named Ferguson, who stowed his case near his feet. The arms dealer had a dark mole on one cheek, pale skin taut on a skinny frame, and close-cropped light hair. "I'm glad we can finish this deal tonight."

"I'm aware of the problem," Diego said.

Their waitress came over, but Ferguson said he didn't want anything. Once the girl had departed, Diego said, "I have your money," and reached into his jacket.

"Not so fast."

Kevin O'Rourke joined the table, grabbing a chair of his own and wedging it between Diego and Ferguson. O'Rourke continued, "This deal isn't done until all bids are considered, right, Ferguson?"

"I already have a deal with him," Ferguson said.

"But I deserve the chance. The free market isn't dead yet. What are they paying you?"

Diego said, "I suggest you excuse yourself before we make a scene here, *mi amigo.* Nobody wants a scene."

"Maybe you don't," O'Rourke said, "but I don't mind a little honest shooting now and then. Keeps my fingers limber." To Ferguson, "Whatever their offer is, I'll give you ten percent more. I have cash."

"And what happens to my reputation?" Ferguson said.

O'Rourke laughed.

Diego said, "I hope you didn't come here alone."

O'Rourke raised an eyebrow. "Got backup, yeah? Nice move, love. I'm not alone, either. Got a man at the bar, and he likes to shoot, too. Got another man down the way. Looks like we have a bit of a stalemate. It's up to you, Ferguson, to break the tie, and I suggest you side with your countrymen."

Ferguson said to Diego, "The case is yours."

Diego pulled a thick envelope out of his jacket. "And

this is yours."

Ferguson took the money and stowed it in his jacket. To O'Rourke, "The deal is done, regardless of what you do next."

O'Rourke's arm flashed to his left armpit; a flash and an explosion came from Diego's side, and O'Rourke slumped dead in his chair. Ferguson hollered and dove for the floor. Diego scooted back, bringing his arm up from under the table as he rose to his feet. His smoking automatic tracked to a man at the bar, who hauled two pistols from behind his back.

Elsa and Pike turned over their table. The hardwood and glasses hit the floor with a crash that shook the walls, and the man with the twin auto pistols turned to them and fired, his rounds striking and splintering the table. Elsa stayed low, her knees on the wood floor, and took out her gun. She aimed for a second man at the far end of the bar who was pointing a pistol their way. Pike fired twice. Sean Collins, with his twin pistols, jerked with each impact, then Pike fired twice more. As Collins went down, he thumped his head against the edge of the bar. Timmy Blaine fired only once, nicking the overturned table, then Elsa shot him in the chest.

Diego, already at the entrance with the case, ignored the screams of other patrons and shouted, "Come on!"

Pike grabbed Elsa's hand and hauled her out of there.

Pike ran a red light and a traffic camera flashed. He didn't slow down, whipping the car onto a highway on-ramp and pressing the accelerator closer to the floor. The engine responded with a surge of power.

Elsa was on her knees in the back seat, looking out the rear window, pistol still in hand. Pike glanced at her in the rearview mirror and noted how the seat of her slacks stretched nicely over her rear end.

"You're offering a great view," he said, "but I think we're okay."

Diego, in the passenger seat, stifled a laugh. The case rested on his lap. "Nice driving."

"Thanks."

Elsa rotated, dropped into the seat, and fastened her seatbelt.

"Almost bought the farm back there," Pike said.

"We did fine," Diego said. "We got the case. Ferguson got paid."

"I didn't see him walk out of there."

"His fate is not our concern," Diego said. "We need to get back to the airport and aboard the jet."

"Tell me there will be a hot shower wherever we'll end up," Pike said. "No offense, but the jet—"

Diego laughed. "I understand, *mi amigo.* You will be accommodated, I promise."

Pike drove on with his jaw clenched.

Not much longer.

Then the reckoning.

Elsa watched the back of Pike's head as he drove, moving easily around other cars as they headed back to the airport. She'd been with a few men in her life, but none like him. None had ever grabbed her the way he had when Diego gave the order to exit the bar. He could have provided cover for her, but no, he'd grabbed her hand, pulling her tightly to him as he ran because there was danger around them and he wanted her out of there as fast as possible. And he shielded her with his body, just in case.

She put her gun in her purse and let out a breath. Nobody spoke.

His air of confidence had attracted her to him in the first place. Unlike her boss and Diego, Pike wasn't trying to impress anybody. What you saw you got. He delivered what he said he could deliver, and his results spoke for themselves. Much of that, she knew, came from his age, but it was a quality few other men possessed, one she appreciated and wanted very much in a companion.

Elsa's heart skipped as she realized she was in love with John Pike. She turned to look out at the passing scenery. She was glad for the silence. She wanted her thoughts uninterrupted as she tried to figure out what her feelings meant and what she could do about it.

CHAPTER THIRTY

Stiletto remembered his last visit to Vienna had included no time for sightseeing, and this would be no different.

He and Nikki had arrived via a commercial flight in the afternoon, and a Trust car driven by a local contact whisked them downtown to the Palais Hansen Kempinski. It was a very upscale hotel close to the center of the city, where the unofficial intelligence group had secured two adjoining rooms under a corporate cover name.

There they waited until the other two members of Scott's team arrived. The general had sent a crew Scott had only worked with off and on.

David Sharke led the way, carrying a heavy case full of equipment. He was joined by Matt Reece, carrying his own case, which he banged on the doorjamb as he entered.

Both were around the same age as Stiletto, with differing hairstyles. Sharke and Reece were very fit, and experts at their jobs, according to General Ike. Reece was the shooter for when the dangerous stuff started. Sharke was the surveillance expert and usually held court in a computer-and-camera-laden van.

Stiletto introduced Nikki Fortune only as his "associate," and Sharke and Reece shook hands with the young woman.

Stiletto directed them to chairs around the table near the window, where he had set up bratwurst, sauerkraut, grilled veggies, and other eats on the table. Amazing aromas filled the room, and it was impossible to resist after their long flights. As they loaded plates, Stiletto booted a laptop and plugged a USB cable into the computer and the other end into the television. He sat in a chair with the computer on his lap.

"I'll go over this as fast as I can," Scott said as the room filled with the sounds of chewing. "It's a typical op, but we have one of our own in the enemy camp. That makes matters a little sensitive."

"Any communications?" Sharke asked with his mouth full.

"Swallow your sausage," Stiletto said.

Sharke swallowed.

Stiletto explained about the cell phone and the exchange he'd had with somebody he believed to be missing CIA agent John Pike, but there had been nothing since the **Stand by** text. If Sharke or Reece disagreed with him, they didn't voice the opinion, nor did their expressions betray their thoughts.

Stiletto moved on with the briefing. A couple of keystrokes brought the face of Morgan Lane onto the television.

"Our target. Her name is Morgan Lane. Arms dealer. We suspect she'll be selling canisters of a chemical weapon to at least two people, one of whom is John Pike."

Stiletto explained they had no idea what type of chemical weapon was being offered for sale, but they needed to secure the containers for destruction under proper protocols.

"Where is Lane hiding?" Sharke said.

"She has a home outside the city," Stiletto said, "but she spends most of her time here." The picture on the television changed once again to show the frontage of a sprawling casino/hotel resort. "We think it's a front for money laundering and to give her a respectable cover."

"Who's going in?"

Stiletto said, "I will. We don't know when Pike and his crew are arriving. We're not sure if they're meeting at the casino or at Lane's home or somewhere else. We need to know where the exchange is taking place, and we need to be there before the rest of them."

"I have a few toys that will help," Sharke said.

Sharke unzipped one of his cases. He took out a small plastic box and lifted the lid.

"Very small listening devices," he said. "Not much bigger than a thumbnail, as you can see. Adhesive backing, so it will stick pretty much anywhere."

"Detectable?" Stiletto said. He leaned close to examine the units.

"That's the beauty of these. They're active as soon as you place them, but they shut off when they sense a counter-signal."

"These can't be totally unknown. Surely somebody is trying to counteract them."

"Prototypes." Sharke tapped the case.

"How did you get them?"

Sharke winked. He put the case away and removed a tablet computer. "Monitor and record on this unit. You can listen and play *Candy Crush* at the same time."

"I prefer *Panda Pop*."

Sharke put the tablet away and opened a shaving kit. He showed Stiletto the electric razor inside. "There's one for each of us in case Lane tries the same tricks with us. Sweep the room to see if she plants anything."

"Can I shave with it?"

"Nope." Sharke put the kit away. "Now let's modify a cell phone."

Sharke, using a small screwdriver, finished adding a new chip into the back of a cell phone. Stiletto, Nikki, and Reece stood beside the table, watching him. Sharke slapped the back cover on and handed the phone to Scott.

"Get this as close as you can to Lane's phone, and that

chip will duplicate everything she has on her cell and become a clone. We'll hear every call she makes."

"Email and text?"

"Yes, but not in real-time."

"How long of a delay?" Stiletto said.

"Maybe ten minutes, depending on how much data
needs to transfer."

"Ten minutes could mean the difference—"

"Nothing we can do about it, Scott."

"Okay."

Nikki jabbed Stiletto in the arm. "Let's go shopping."

"I can get my own stuff."

"If you pick something wrong, Lane will notice."

"Nikki—"

"Don't argue with me, come on."

"Let's not spend all my money."

Nikki started for the door. "Oh, I'm going to bankrupt
you."

Stiletto exchanged a helpless glance with Sharke and
Reece before following Nikki out of the room. As the elevator descended, they looked at each other. Nikki's grin
and the gleam in her eye told him he was in for quite a
makeover.

CHAPTER THIRTY-ONE

Stiletto took some time to wander the resort. Tennis courts, swimming pool, shops, spas—everything a modern resort required. He was wearing a fancier suit than he would have liked, but coupled with a fresh haircut that Nikki had also insisted on, Stiletto looked like a perfect international playboy with an edge.

He spent most of the day in the casino, playing various table games, winning and losing, making his face known to the pit bosses and staying in view of security cameras.

His plan for approaching Morgan Lane didn't include finding her at the casino. He had a more direct approach in mind.

After the sun set, he went about making the plan happen.

Another pair of eyes watched Scott Stiletto.

Sergei Vasilov of the Russian SVR, taking his sweet

time about making a move on Morgan Lane, recognized Stiletto. The American appeared to be checking out the resort, same as he had on his arrival earlier. Sergei mixed with the tourists, as anonymous as any other, using an American accent and a US passport.

He remembered Stiletto as a high-value target of the Kremlin for illegally entering Russia and assisting a group of traitors accused of plotting a coup. Sergei had quietly sided with the coup plotters as well as the American, but he didn't think the time was right to introduce himself.

If he played his cards right, he had the opportunity to terminate Morgan Lane per his assignment, while the Americans escaped with the chemical weapon. *Oops, so sorry, boss. The Yanks got it before me.*

It was a strategy worth thinking about. It was a strategy that, if successfully employed, would accomplish his goals.

The old men in Moscow simply could not get their hands on Sallig Mahfi's weapon.

Scott's plan called for not killing anybody.

This time.

Morgan Lane lived in a mansion outside Vienna, surrounded by a high wall, with a security force in-residence, although not many and not heavily armed. She had to keep a low profile, after all. The best information the Trust had collected said the guards carried only Taser guns and extendable batons.

He followed a mountain road through heavy forest to reach the property. He parked off the road and hiked the rest of the way.

Wearing thick rubber gloves to protect his hands from the glass shards atop the wall, Stiletto climbed up and over, scraping his legs against the top of the wall and stifling a cry as the glass cut into his left thigh. Them were the breaks. He landed on the other side, tossing the gloves away. They landed in nearby bushes.

A motor whirred in the tree to his left. Stiletto looked up—a camera, aimed right at his face. He smiled and waved.

Stiletto marched through the garden, avoiding thorny rose bushes, grabbing two handfuls of loose dirt. Then he found a stone pathway leading to the front porch of the house. He started walking. Already the guard force was massing to meet him. All four of them.

Morgan Lane liked her big garden. A mass of floral wonder of various bright colors and sweet scents surrounded him. The trees seemed like an afterthought, but their leaves rustled in the wind and provided nice shade. And cover, should the trunks be required to stop bullets.

Stiletto examined the welcoming crew. One had a Taser in hand. He was the largest, with a big head full of black hair. The others carried extendable batons and didn't seem all that striking.

Stiletto didn't want to get hit with either weapon. Batons hurt no matter where they struck, and if you wanted your day to end early, mess around with a Taser. Stiletto would rather get shot in the butt with a .45 than take the prongs of a taser.

But sometimes you had to take the hits to get to the top, and nothing was going to stop him from getting into the house to meet Morgan Lane when she returned home for the evening.

The Taser, for certain, had to be avoided. That man was going down first.

"You need to leave the property," Taser Man said.

"I bet you say that to all the guys."

Taser Man was about to say something more when Stiletto stepped within range. He tossed both handfuls of dirt in Taser Man's face, getting the wanted reaction when it hit him. Stiletto sent a kick into his stomach as he grabbed for the taser, snatching the weapon from the man's grip as he hit the ground.

The other three converged. Stiletto fired the taser into the chest of the man closest to his left. The prongs punched through the fabric of his shirt and embedded in the flesh of his chest. The man yelled and went into convulsions.

One of the last two swung at Scott. He ducked under the swing, but the third attacked too, kicking Scott's feet out from under him. Scott hit the ground, and somebody kicked him in the belly. He grabbed the ankle and twisted as it drew back, and the guard fell off balance and landed next to Stiletto. The last guard stepped back as Scott smashed the guard next to him in the head once, twice. Then he jumped up and blocked the swing of the last man's baton with his left forearm. He jabbed the guard in the throat with a two-finger strike, then brought a foot into the man's crotch.

All four men were spread out on the ground, groaning, the fight long out of them.

Stiletto, gasping, almost had no fight left in him either. He returned to Taser Man, punched him a second time, and grabbed the keys from the pocket of the man's slacks.

The front door was unlocked, because how else would the crew get back inside? Stiletto sauntered into the house and took in the ornate foyer. He ignored most of the decorations as he moved to the large living room off the front entrance. Selecting a leather couch, he dropped onto one end and spent a few minutes catching his breath.

When he finally resumed normal breathing, still keeping an eye on the four guards in the yard through the front window, he removed a cigar container and lighter from the inside pocket of his jacket. The H. Upmann 1844 would taste good after that workout. He started puffing, waiting for the return of Morgan Lane.

Morgan Lane tried to relax as her driver left the casino and made the trip home. There was a lot on her mind. Having a cache of chemical weapons was enough to give her stomach problems. Perhaps that was why she'd been chewing on antacids since the start of this assignment from Harrison Joule.

The payday would be worth the discomfort, however. Morgan Lane always kept her eyes on the prize.

She'd spent most of her life in the underground anarchist scene, only "going legit" about a decade earlier. That had led to her position at the casino, where she'd turned the operation into a way to launder money for various clients. She also handled contraband sales on an as-needed basis, but when Joule had contacted her about collecting a pair of canisters containing chemical weapons, she'd realized she'd either grown very big in the world or was circling the drain.

That kind of weapon brought heat from every Western intelligence organization.

But the containers of the deadly bacteria wouldn't be in her possession much longer. Joule's representatives were on their way, and presently she could go back to her normal activities and not fuss so much.

She saw the prostrate forms in her yard. The leader of the guard force, Angus Barrett, who was bigger than the rest, and supposedly as strong as an ox, was trying to get the rest on their feet. She ordered the driver to stop well before the house and jumped out of the car to find out what the hell was going on.

She hoped they had a good story.

Her twin bodyguards emerged from the car with her, drawing weapons. She wasn't sure who they were going to shoot.

CHAPTER THIRTY-TWO

"Barrett, what the hell?"

Barrett held up a hand as he plucked taser prongs from the chest of one of her men. After he'd helped the woozy man to his feet, he said, "Inside the house, ma'am."

"What inside the house?"

"The guy who did this to us."

"One guy?"

Barrett's big head went up and down in a nod.

"Oh," Morgan Lane said. "This I got to see."

The twin bodyguards stayed behind her as she marched to the front door, her heels clicking on the pavement. She smelled cigar smoke right away.

"You better put out that stinky-ass cigar, whoever you are," she said to the man on her couch. "And get off my couch!"

Scott Stiletto grinned. He'd heard about Morgan Lane's fiery temper and was glad to see firsthand that the reports had not been inaccurate.

"Morgan Lane, I presume?" Stiletto said.

"Who are you?" She put her hands on her hips. The twins stepped to the side and leveled their pistols at Scott.

Stiletto puffed on the H. Upmann. "Tell your boy-friends to put the rods away. I'm not armed."

"You looking for a fancy way to commit suicide or something?"

"My apologies for busting in here the way I did, but I didn't think I could just walk up to you at the casino."

Morgan Lane dismissed the twins, telling them to go back outside and help take care of Barrett and the others. The twins complied without comment. Morgan Lane did not make a move to sit down.

"This better be good."

Stiletto said, "My name is Michael Hayden."

"What does that mean to me?"

"I have a business proposition I know you'll appreciate."

"You looking for a job?"

"Yeah."

"I could use somebody on the janitorial staff. Is that your proposition?"

Stiletto laughed.

"Let's stop the joking," he said. "We both know the score, Ms. Morgan. You buy and sell items that are then put up for sale to various people around the world. That includes guns. I have a crate of US M-16s I'd like to sell—at a negotiated price, of course."

"So what?"

"These are M-16s that are being decommissioned and put into storage. My contacts and I are taking a few of them off the inventory sheets. Nobody's going to know they're missing. It's all profit to you."

The woman eyed Stiletto with curiosity. "I'll have to make a few calls before we can talk further, Mr. Hayden."

"Great. Finally."

"I'm going to have to check you out, you realize?"

"Of course."

"And my people aren't going to be happy with you."

"If you want to make money on what I'm selling, I better stay in one piece."

"Put out that cigar."

"I'll take it with me." Stiletto rose form the couch. He approached Morgan Land and extended a hand. She was shorter than him by an inch or two. She folded her arms and gave him an unblinking stare.

"We'll shake when I know you're not trying to bust me."

Stiletto winked. He left the house through the front door. The guards were back on their feet, still recovering from the fight, and Scott marched past with a wave. He walked along the stone pathway through the garden to the front gate, where he let himself out. He didn't look back to find out if Morgan Lane was watching him from the porch.

Back to the hotel to regroup.

Stiletto skipped further casino play for a seat at a bar. He ordered a Makers-and-Coke. He did not select a corner table despite his better judgment, relying on the bar's mirror to help him cover his back.

He took out his cell and called Nikki.

"How did it go?"

Stiletto gave her the update, adding, "They'll be watching me. Do I stay away from you guys or what?"

There was a quick discussion on the other end, then Nikki came back on the line. "She'll know you'll need help. I don't think it will hurt."

"Okay, but let's wait until she digs into the Michael Hayden cover and feels better about this deal."

A trio entered the bar, talking and laughing. Stiletto saw them in the mirror. All three were males, thin and muscular with short haircuts. Too tanned for average tourists. Soldier-types? He'd never have been able to afford a resort like this when he was in the service. Perhaps they were more of Morgan Lane's people sent to watch him?

"She has people all over here," Stiletto said and described the new arrivals.

"It's never easy, is it?"

Stiletto hung up, finished his drink, and ordered another. The Hayden cover was a safe one, that of a small-fry international arms dealer, one who could never hit a big score but moved plenty of small-arms and never had any complaints about the quality of the equipment he moved.

He wasn't sure he wanted to go back to his room yet. Maybe they were searching while he was drinking. He decided to keep drinking and let them have some time to poke around.

CHAPTER THIRTY-THREE

Stiletto checked his watch.

Enough time had passed. He finished his third Makers-and-Coke and paid up. As he left, he made brief eye contact with the trio. For sure; he knew soldiers when he saw them. Back in his room, he sat up in bed and selected a comedy from the pay movies on offer.

A knock on the door distracted him. He muted the television and took the .45 from beside the bed before he answered the door.

Morgan Lane stood there, holding a bottle of Russian Standard vodka. A small sparkly purse hung from her right shoulder.

"Is that a gun in your hand, or are you just happy to see me?"

"What are you doing here?" he said.

"Thought I'd see if you wanted a nightcap." She held up the bottle and smiled.

Stiletto stepped back and let her in. He tossed the pistol on the bed and retrieved glasses from the bathroom. She had the bottle open and the purse on the dresser by the time he returned. She filled both glasses, took one, and offered a toast.

"Here's to crime."

They drank and sat at the table. Stiletto scooted his chair closer to her.

"Tell me," he said, "why you're visiting me after slaving at this casino all day?"

"I checked you out, and many sources vouch for you. I can't exactly send one of my representatives from the house, because you beat the shit out of all of them. The people I have around here aren't suited for the sort of conversation we need to have, so I decided to come over myself."

"You'd prefer a close-up look to see whether I'm a spy?"

"If you want something done right, *right?*"

"Sure."

"Nature of the business, darling." She laughed and swallowed some vodka.

Stiletto drank some vodka too. It was strong but smooth.

"Uh-huh."

The purse began to vibrate.

"What's that?"

"My phone."

"Oh, really? How nice."

"I'll ignore it."

"What if it's one of your people and they found out I'm a spy?"

"I have a gun in there, too, I'll just kill you myself."

"How nice."

They drank. The phone stopped vibrating.

"Don't let it bother you. Here, your glass is low."

She topped off Stiletto's drink.

"Why are there so many soldiers here?" he said.

"You could tell? Of course, you could." She laughed. "I mean, you might be low man on the totem pole in terms of gun-running, but you know your stuff."

Presently, they drained the bottle, and Stiletto left the chair. He moved behind her and started massaging her neck and shoulders.

"Ooooh, magic fingers," she said.

"Where did you grow up?"

"Bonn."

"Tell me about growing up in Bonn."

"It snowed a lot. Mmmmmm, that's nice. Where did you grow up?"

"I don't remember."

"Ha-ha, liar." She jumped up and poked him in the chest. "I told, now you tell. Come on, tell." She gave him a shove.

Stiletto grabbed her arms, spun her around, and slammed her against the wall. She let out a little yelp, and Stiletto kissed her hard. She responded, pressing her warm lips against his. Stiletto ran his hands along her hips and rear, pulling her closer. He turned her around again and shoved her toward the bed.

He wasn't sure it was the sort of up-close review she had in mind, but she didn't argue.

Stiletto lay awake, staring at the ceiling mostly because Morgan Lane snored like a pig.

Her phone was in the purse, still on the dresser, about five feet away from him. The clone phone doctored by Reece was in the pocket of his trousers, currently on the carpet. He rolled out of bed and put his bare feet on the soft carpet, then found his trousers and put them on. He left his belt loose, and the ends dangled in front of him. Heading for the bathroom, he activated the clone phone and placed it on the dresser. A red line appeared on the screen and began a slow crawl from left to right.

He shut the bathroom door and waited for a few minutes, then flushed the toilet, and wandered back toward the bed. The red line on the clone phone had turned green and filled the bar, so he dropped it back in his pants, removed them once again, and slid back under the covers.

Morgan still snored.

Stiletto let out a quiet laugh.

He awoke again with the barrel of a gun jabbed in his crotch.

"Um…"

"Make and model, quick."

"Smith & Wesson Model 60, stainless."

She laughed and pulled the gun away from his privates. "Very good."

"Hell of a wakeup call."

She placed the revolver on the nightstand on her side of the bed.

"Tell me more about your guns. We kinda forgot about those."

Stiletto's pulse was still racing. He took a deep breath and shifted a little. "I have three crates total, with one here in Knokke to show as a sample. Stolen right out of inventory on their way to storage. Nobody will notice."

"Uh-huh. When can I see them?"

"As soon as today."

"Good." She rolled over and straddled him.

"Shouldn't we shower first?"

She laughed, grinding against him. "Don't be silly."

Sharke said, "Here he comes."

Scott Stiletto approached the table in the outdoor seating area of the hotel's main restaurant. Nikki, Sharke, and Reece sat in the shadow of the building so the sun didn't beat on them.

Stiletto took the empty seat. Nikki sat to his left. He said good morning and updated the team. The waitress interrupted to take their orders, and he continued, "She wants to see us at her place this afternoon with the samples."

"Where are we going to get a crate of US rifles?" Nikki said.

"We can let headquarters figure that out," Reece said. "We can whip up a sample case of M-16s and M-4s and whatever else we need."

Stiletto continued, "I'll make arrangements for the three of you to show the guns."

"What's your agenda?" Nikki asked Scott.

"Hang around and try and bug her office." Stiletto took out the cloned cell phone and passed it to Sharke. "Is it working?"

Sharke took a moment to examine the phone's settings. "It's working. She hasn't used her phone so far today."

"The one woman who isn't always on her phone," Stiletto said. "Nice."

CHAPTER THIRTY-FOUR

Nikki sat quietly beside Sharke as he drove the rental car into the warehouse parking lot. Reece sat in the back. Nobody had spoken much during the drive, and for Nikki, that was fine. She hadn't wanted Scott to stay behind, but he didn't want to incur the wrath of any of her banged-up bodyguards and put the deal at risk.

She didn't mind. She was getting along great with Sharke and Reece and decided the Trust had some good people working for it. She wanted to tell them that if the gig didn't work out, they could work for her.

Reece had phoned the local Trist contacts and request-ed assistance with their "arms deal," which had netted them the promise of a padded hard case containing three M-16 rifles. The weapons would suffice as a sample and prove to Morgan Lane that they were the real deal.

The warehouse had office space in front and looked to be in relatively good repair. Sharke drove around to the back, where a blue panel van waited beside a sliding door. Two men waited inside the van. Sharke, Nikki, and Reece exited the car, and Reece introduced the two Trust agents in the van.

The Trust contacts opened the back of the van to reveal the long hard case, which they opened. The three M-16 rifles were nestled inside. Reece did all the talking as the embassy men explained that the weapons had to be brought back in the exact same condition they were in now.

They traded vehicles. The contacts drove off in the rental, while Nikki, Sharke, and Reece climbed into the van.

Nikki's pistol dug into the small of her back, and she shifted uncomfortably. The van's suspension wasn't the best, and they seemed to hit every bump in the road.

"The glamor of undercover work," she said.

"Just don't break the other stuff you're carrying," Reece said from the back.

The "other stuff" consisted of two of the thumbnail micro-bugs, which rode in a small plastic case stowed in the left pocket of her jeans. An untucked loose shirt helped hide her pistol.

Two bugs weren't a lot, but they figured strategic placement was better than full coverage.

But they had to get inside Morgan Lane's house first.

The ride didn't take long. Sharke followed a two-lane highway that eventually rose into forest-covered hills.

Sharke turned right, seemingly into the forest, following an access road that was overgrown on either side. When the area ahead cleared, Morgan Lane's single-level mansion awaited behind its protective wall.

Sharke followed the circular driveway. A weeping angel statue surrounded by colorful flowers filled the spot in the center of the driveway. The angel stood straight, wings folded, head bowed, hands over her face.

"Those statues give me the creeps," Nikki said.

Sharke stopped the van and pulled the handbrake.

"You've been quiet, David," Reece said.

"The quiet ones are the smartest," Sharke shot back.

The front door of the mansion opened.

Morgan Lane, wearing a wrinkled pink skirt over a yellow top, with her twin bodyguards on either side stepped out.

Nikki, Sharke, and Reece climbed out of the van. Sharke and Reece stayed beside the vehicle while Nikki approached Lane.

"Ms. Lane, I presume?"

"That's me. Scott didn't tell me to expect a woman."

"That's men for you," Nikki said. "I brought my associates to help with the sample case."

"Let's see it."

Nikki led Lane to the van, where Sharke and Reece opened the rear doors and hauled the hard case to the edge of the bumper. Sharke flipped the locks and raised the lid. The flat black M-16 rifles, with their dull finish, sat unassumingly in the case.

Morgan Lane stepped close to examine the rifles, then hefted one, noting the U.S. property markings.

"Very good." She put the rifle back where she'd found it.

"How many crates?"

"Three. Thirty grand per crate, twenty guns each."

"Way too high. That's fifteen hundred per gun."

"Yeah, guns the military won't miss and won't come looking for."

"Twenty thousand per crate."

"Twenty-eight," Nikki countered.

Morgan Lane folded her arms. "Do you think I'm made of money?"

"You'll be able to mark these up, and you know it."

"Nobody will pay that much."

"These guns are clean."

"Twenty-two thousand."

"Twenty-five or we're done."

Morgan Lane let out a sigh, frowning as she looked at the rifles once more.

Nikki's pulse quickened. If they couldn't get into the house—

Morgan turned her attention back to Dodge. "Twenty-four."

"Now it's twenty-six. I'm not giving them away."

She kept her eyes on Nikki, who remained stoic. Not a muscle in her face moved.

Morgan Lane stuck out her hand. "Twenty-five."

"Deal." They shook. "I can deliver the other two in

forty-eight hours."

"Make it seventy-two. I have other guests arriving first."

"Good to know," Nikki said. "Let's celebrate with a drink inside."

"Not today," Morgan Lane said. "Bring Scott to the casino tonight, and we'll all have a drink then."

Nikki pressed her lips together.

"Our business is done," Morgan Lane said. "I expect the guns will arrive on time with no problems." She turned and started back for the house. The twin dutifully followed.

Nikki cursed as Sharke and Reece locked the back of the van, and the trio got back inside.

"I think she got pissed at the end," Reece said as Sharke drove back to the main road.

"She lost the negotiation," Nikki said. "Maybe I should have let her win."

"We still have her phone," Reese pointed out.

"We do, don't we?" Nikki said.

CHAPTER THIRTY-FIVE

Stiletto turned to the back page of the *Financial Times* and shot a passing glance across the top edge of the paper. He sat with his legs stretched out on a lounge chair, chilled drink to his right. He wore the requisite shorts, but also a long-sleeved shirt that was only buttoned at the bottom. He might have been a little out of place, but he wouldn't get the stares his scars might attract.

The pool was full of kids splashing around, while adults kept to the outer edges under umbrellas. It was a warm day with a nice breeze. In other words, none of the umbrellas would topple over if Mother Nature sneezed too hard. The back of the hotel loomed, some guests skipping the pool to lounge on their balconies. They had the better view.

Across the pool from where Stiletto lay, a bar was ready to cater to one's alcoholic whims, and leaning against the bar was a big man, fully dressed, who couldn't keep his eyes off Stiletto. Stiletto might have been flattered, except he knew the attention carried certain lethal overtones.

Angus Barrett. Morgan Lane's "Taser Man."

Stiletto returned to his reading.

His cell rang. He put the paper down to answer.

"Yes?"

"Where are you?" Nikki said.

"Relaxing by the pool with a Long Island Iced Tea. Come join me."

"Is that a reward for a mission accomplished?"

"Hardly. I've had that chrome-dome bodyguard's eyes on me since I left the room today. I thought hanging back would keep me *out* of trouble."

"Hang on."

Stiletto waited. He couldn't hear Nikki or the others above the noise in the pool area. Then Nikki came back on the line.

"Get up here. She's on the phone."

Stiletto shut the door. Nikki, Reece, and Sharke sat at the table with the cloned phone and a laptop in front of them. Sharke's fingers tapped the keys.

"What happened?" Stiletto said. He took a seat on the corner of the bed.

"She finally got a call, and it's gold," Reece said.

Sharke opened a window with a sound file and played back the recording.

Morgan Lane's voice: "Hello?"

"It's me."

"Yes, Marco. No problems, I hope?"

"No, we're actually early. I know you weren't expecting us for another couple of days, but can we move up our time?"

"I have everything ready. My place, tonight, midnight. Will that work?"

"We'll be there."

Sharke stopped the playback.

Nikki exchanged looks with Stiletto.

"We got 'em," he stated.

"We'll find a cozy spot off the road and wait for them to come to us," Nikki said.

Nikki's "cozy" spot on the road was a cutout. Sharke backed the van as far into the brush as he could go. He and Nikki occupied the van. Stiletto and Reece had gone ahead, loaded for the recon, to report on what they saw of the property.

The black van blended with the darkness outside, the enveloping shadows from the trees and brush adding to the camouflage. As long as nobody used the cutout, they'd be fine. Nikki and Sharke moved into the back of the van, where there were two chairs in front of monitors and radio equipment. Nikki dropped into the hard chair and scooted close to the panels, watching over Sharke's shoulder and trying not to get too close.

Sharke activated a computer and started a scan of the area. Nikki watched his fingers move and information appear on the monitor. It cycled so fast she couldn't read all of it. Sharke stopped and pointed out three lines of numbers, two digits separated by a period, then three digits, another period, and two more numbers.

"She has wireless security cameras," Sharke said. "At three points on the property."

"Can you tap into them?"

"Sure."

Sharke's fingers flew across the keyboard. After a few minutes, three of the monitors before them lit up with black-and-white footage of the property. Nikki watched the troopers making their rounds. They carried pistols and submachine guns.

"I found some recorded footage," Sharke accounted. "Watch the center monitor."

The picture changed to the inside of a room, where Morgan Lane met with two clients, both men, neither of whom Nikki recognized.

"Can you copy this?"

"In progress," Sharke said.

Sharke sped through the footage. A series of clients passed through the office, none staying more than a few minutes, and none exchanging money for goods. Nikki looked at the faces. Most of them were men, and none of them were her father.

And then...

The couple entered the office, the man letting the woman enter first. The woman was shorter than her male companion, and Nikki felt her pulse quicken. When the man glanced up at the camera as he completed a scan of the room, Nikki put a hand to her mouth. It was Scott's friend John Pike, and no mistake.

"Nikki?" Sharke said.

"I know."

"Do we tell him?"

"I will."

They watched the silent video. John Pike, Elsa Suba, and Morgan Lane conversed for about fifteen minutes, almost as if they were a married couple consulting with a real estate agent. Buying a chemical weapon to kill thousands was that mundane. They'd probably pick up cat food on the way home.

When Pike and the woman left, Nikki asked Sharke to make sure he saved the footage in a separate file.

"Already done," Sharke said as hc completed the keystrokes.

"Let's go back to the live feed."

The monitor switched back to what it had shown before: more of the property, and it looked like the same number of guards still freely roamed.

Nikki had an earbud in her left ear so she could hear and talk to Stiletto and Reece, but so far, the radio had been silent. She wondered how Scott was doing.

The automatic carbine strapped across his back poked through Stiletto's shirt, and the ground was a little wet and cold, but otherwise, it was a good night for a snatch-and-grab. Stiletto and Reece, up the road from where the van sat, planted small charges on the shoulder of the road, which sank into the dirt with the help of spikes extending from the bottom of the rectangular charge. Stiletto would trigger the bombs as the car containing John Pike and the other buyers approached. The explosives put out a low-level blast, designed to destroy front tires rather than whole vehicles. With the bombs set, he joined Reece deep in the shadows of the brush. Scott held the trigger for the bombs.

Stiletto breathed heavily but slowly as he settled down after the effort, the chill of the night cooling the sweat on his face and neck.

He faced the road, listening.

Now they had to wait.

CHAPTER THIRTY-SIX

"Is she expecting trouble?" Pike said.

Diego steered the car through the checkpoint at the front gate and onto the curved driveway leading to the house ahead. The house was one-story, a set of steps leading to a porch with an overhang supported by a stone pillar on either side.

"Why do you ask?"

Elsa supplied the answer. "Extra troops. An obvious number of extra troops."

"She has the chem weapon on-site," Diego said. "Of course, she wants extra security."

Pike took out his pistol and checked it.

"Paranoid, *mi amigo*?"

"Something isn't right here," Pike said. He heard Elsa in the back seat check her gun as well.

Diego took a deep breath. "Don't be offended if I say I hope you're wrong."

"I'm not. I hope I am too."

Diego stopped the car in front of the house. Two troopers approached the vehicle as Morgan Lane exited the house to stand atop the porch steps.

The three of them exited the car. One of the troopers motioned for Pike to open his jacket, but Lane called, "Never mind. They can keep their weapons."

They crossed the tiled entry hall to Lane's office, the cozy, dark-paneled room they'd visited before. This time, propped in a corner, sat yet another steel case. Lane knelt in front of the case and opened the locks. Raising the lid, she showed them the two canisters inside.

They were small canisters, stainless steel, about eight inches long and maybe two inches in diameter. Brightly polished. Flat at either end. The canisters would fit perfectly into the warheads they'd collected previously.

Pike felt his pulse surge. He took a breath to cover.

Diego produced an envelope from his jacket. "The balance of our agreement."

Lane closed the case, rose, took the envelope, and rifled the cash inside. She said. "I'm going to send some men down the hill with you in a separate vehicle."

"Sounds fine," Diego said, appearing calm. Pike almost bought it.

"Then I won't keep you any longer." She smiled.

Pike picked up the case and carried it out. He moved quickly.

Diego and Elsa matched his stride.

Diego left the property a little faster than he'd arrived, not letting his foot off the accelerator as the car met each curve. He twisted the wheel expertly, keeping the car in the lane.

"I'll never doubt you again, *mi amigo*."

"I'll be happier when we're back on the jet."

"The SUV with the gun crew is staying about three car-lengths back," Elsa reported.

Lane had loaded the other vehicle with four troopers, all armed with automatic rifles.

"It's not our back I'm concerned about," Pike said.

The night surrounded them, the sides of the road pitch-black, only the headlights piercing the darkness before them. Pike took out his gun and clicked off the safety.

Asphalt rolled beneath the car, the broken white dividing line flashing under the blaze of the headlamps. Pike scanned left and right. His head did not stop moving. When he yelled for Diego to stop, it was already too late.

Twin blasts flashed from the roadside, and the car spun, tires screeching. The final violent jolt knocked everybody silly. The back windows shattered and shards of glass flew in all directions, nicking Pike's neck. Elsa screamed again. The side airbags deployed with a bang and Pike cursed, slashing at them uselessly with his pistol. Smoke and a putrid scent of burned rubber shot through the dash vents.

"Out!" Diego yelled, opening his door and rolling onto the pavement.

Pike crawled across the front seat, landing hard on the grimy asphalt.

Two men in black with automatic weapons emerged from the side of the road and jogged toward them, shouting commands. In English. Americans. Pike grit his teeth. *No, you idiots!*

The gun crew's SUV accelerated around a curve, its bright beams like a spotlight on the two commandos.

When the explosions flashed and the car spun out, Stiletto and Reece bolted from hiding.

Nikki's voice crackled over Stiletto's earpiece: "There's another vehicle coming!"

Stiletto kept his focus forward, sighting down the barrel of his automatic rifle as two figures crawled out of the vehicle. *Males. One of them John Pike!* Stiletto began yelling commends. *Get away from the car. Throw away your weapons. Hands in the air!*

He saw Pike look at him, his eyes pleading. Stiletto frowned. Then the headlights of an onrushing SUV turned his shadow into an arrow that stretched along the roadway.

"Incoming!" Reece yelled.

Automatic weapons cracked as Reece engaged the arriving vehicle. Stiletto dashed for Pike's car but stopped short when the woman, Elsa Suba, leaned out the busted back window.

Stiletto dropped flat. Elsa fired once. The bullet split the air over his head. He rolled as she fired again and again, the rounds whining off the asphalt. Stiletto regained the shoulder, crawling for cover as Pike and the other man, a Hispanic by the look of him, ushered Elsa out of the car and across to the opposite side of the roadway and the thick brush there, using their wrecked car for additional cover.

Reece's voice said in Stiletto's ear, "We got four hostiles in the SUV!" A burst of gunfire. "Now three!"

"Our subjects are behind their car, and the woman at least is armed," Stiletto said, swinging his sights on the SUV the three gunmen clustered around. One lay in the road, obviously dead.

Stiletto fired, the flash from his muzzle bright in the night, and knocked down another gunman. The other two shuffled away from the SUV, and Reece started to pursue. One gunman rolled a grenade across the asphalt. Reece saw the grenade too late and the blast wiped him out, the flash lighting up the roadway. Stiletto threw up an arm to protect his face and rolled into the roadside dirt. Bits of shrapnel rained down on him.

"Scott!" Nikki screamed.

"I'm here," he said. He left the side of the road and charged across the asphalt, stopping at the front corner of the gun crew's SUV. From the wrecked car, Elsa Suba winged a shot at him, nicking the windshield. Stiletto sent a burst their way, pivoting back as the surviving members of the gun crew realized where he was. Stiletto moved around the driver's side of the SUV and fired one stream of shots over the hood, then shifted his aim and fired another. Both gunmen crashed back into the foliage.

Stiletto dropped to one knee, reloaded, and turned his attention to the primary target.

"We're coming, Scott!" Nikki said.

"Take it slow," he told her.

Stiletto took baby steps backward around the rear of the SUV to the bodies of the two gunmen. He patted one down and found a grenade. Stiletto clutched it in his left hand and moved back to the car.

The woman dashed across the street, firing as she moved. Stiletto ducked back. Somebody else opened fire, driving Stiletto farther back. He couldn't see what he was shooting at, and he didn't want to hit Johnny. *Dammit!*

Muzzle flashes winked from either side of the road, the pops of the pistol rounds echoing as the bullets zeroed in on Stiletto. He moved to the rear of the SUV as Nikki's van turned the corner ahead. He held out a hand. Stiletto ran to the van as slugs nicked the ground. David Sharke jumped out on the driver's side, his pistol barking in response to the incoming fire. Stiletto ran past him to slam back against the van. Sharke's head popped, and bits of flesh and bone landed on Stiletto's arm. He let out a yell for Nikki to stay inside as Sharke fell, Stiletto stepping back to avoid his body. Nikki yelled, but he didn't hear. He moved around the back of the van to the passenger side, shouldering his rifle. The woman, Elsa, had run to one of the dead gunmen and grabbed an assault weapon. She held it at hip level and sprayed rounds. Stiletto dropped flat, returning fire as she climbed into the SUV. Part of the rear window shattered as she poked the muzzle of her weapon out, and Pike and the Hispanic used her covering fire as a chance to get into the vehicle.

The engine started. Stiletto fired a shot at the rear wheel, missed, and lunged to his feet. He pulled the pin on the grenade and pitched it overhand. It sailed through the air, landing in front of the car, only to be kicked aside by the tires as the speeding machine went by. The grenade skidded off the road and exploded on the shoulder, sparking a small fire.

Nikki screamed. Stiletto ran around to the other side, where she knelt beside Sharke's body.

"We gotta go!"

He grabbed the back of her shirt and hauled her away from Sharke. "Get in! Now! Move it!"

Stiletto drove the van as fast as he dared, taking the curves way too fast. The tires screeched in protest. There was no way to catch up with the SUV, but they also had to put distance between them and the fight. Nikki, on the phone to the general, gave a verbal report, her voice shaking, words coming out in a rush Scott had a hard time following. Stiletto kept his eyes on the road. His pulse raced as he tried to sort out what had happened and how it might have been prevented.

It was the backup gun crew that had done them in, he realized. Take it out of the equation, and they would be riding away with John Pike explaining his side of the story.

Stiletto took it easy through the city streets, his hands tight on the wheel. His clothes were dirty and his face scuffed, but he didn't look injured.

But he was not okay. His mission to prove that John Pike hadn't betrayed his country had encountered a major setback. Pike had been within mere feet of him, and Scott had not only lost him again but his team as well. They had to clean up the mess and try to salvage something from the operation because all they had now was the worst possible scenario: Scott's friend was working with unknown hostiles to acquire chemical weapons for an unknown purpose. He sent off a silent prayer for another text. Anything to keep from thinking the worst.

Otherwise, he had to believe the worst.

Because now the CIA, as General Ike had told him when this nightmare of an assignment began, might have no option but to kill one of their own.

"Where do we ditch the van?" Nikki said.

Stiletto had no answer.

"You awake?"

"We don't," Stiletto finally said. "Take it back to the Trust."

"Are you nuts?"

"We have evidence. We need to get it processed."

Scott swallowed hard. He felt dazed, on autopilot. *His friend was a traitor. But why?* Training was taking over. Stiletto was going through established motions embedded for such emergencies.

He said nothing more and kept driving.

CHAPTER THIRTY-SEVEN

One of the twins drove.

Morgan Lane sat tensely in the back of the sedan, the second of her bodyguards beside her in the back seat. They couldn't go down the mountain; the remains of the gun battle were there, along with the police. They drove higher into the mountains to a road that eventually connected with the main highway, and they followed that route back into Vienna and the hotel.

It wasn't that she felt safe there, but she had items in her office that she needed. She'd be taking a long break from Vienna. Her orders to the remaining security force at the house were to keep everything under control and explain to any cops who wandered by that she wasn't available.

At the hotel, the twins followed her as she exited her private elevator and hurried down a short hallway to a pair of double doors. She took out a key to unlock the doors, but froze, then jumped back, telling the twins, "It's already open. Somebody's in there."

The twins didn't respond verbally. They drew pistols and one kicked the doors open, both dodging back for cover. Morgan Lane dropped behind an end table on one wall.

A voice from her office.

"I suggest we talk, Miss Lane."

Russian accent.

She frowned, peeking over the edge of the table.

"This won't take long, Miss Lane."

Bloody hell, can anybody waltz into my home and office?

The twins looked at her for orders. She drew a finger across her neck. They nodded.

Both men moved swiftly through the doorway with their pistols up.

Two shots, suppressed. The gunfire sounded like a heavy dictionary landing on a desk. Two bodies hit the floor.

Morgan Lane's throat dropped into her stomach.

"My apologies, Miss Lane," the Russian called out. "Please come in. I only want to talk."

She froze in place. Had the team that had killed Sallig Mahfi come for her?

She had no way to summon the hotel security force from the hallway. She needed to get to her desk.

Would she live long enough?

Only one way to find out.

She rose and straightened her clothes. She was going to walk in like a lady and take care of business.

She passed through the doorway and stopped for a sad look at the twins. They'd been good men. Their deaths had been quick, each shot through the forehead.

Morgan Lane raised an eyebrow. "I'm impressed."

She turned to her desk. It was empty. She turned her head to the left. A man with a suppressed SIG-Sauer autoloader sat on the corner couch, legs crossed, wearing a dark suit. He was older than she'd expected.

"Old dogs and old tricks, Miss Lane."

"What do you want?"

"You're going to stand still and answer some questions."

"Who are you?"

"Russian SVR. We almost met in Berlin."

"I figured."

"Where's the chemical agent going?"

"Is that what you want?" she said. "Why not make an offer? No need to kill my people."

"You aren't answering my question, young lady."

"Shoot me and you'll never get an answer to your question, *grandpa*."

The Russian cleared his throat and shifted, but the muzzle of the SIG didn't leave her midsection. One of the twins had dropped his pistol inches from her right foot. She only needed a moment's distraction. Maybe he'd have to get up and pee in the middle of the conversation.

"Tell me what I want to know, Miss Lane."

She folded her arms.

"No."

Sergei Vasilov shook his head in annoyance. He saw the gun at her right foot. She was killing time to find the opportunity to grab the pistol and shoot him.

And he obviously wasn't going to get anywhere with her.

"We're wasting time, Miss Lane."

"Hey, gramps, you waited for me."

"No longer," Vasilov said.

He fired once.

Nikki had been in no mood for her usual post-combat attentions, and Stiletto didn't mind. He wanted to be alone too.

On the road, they had called the local Trust contacts, who had met them in an empty parking lot and taken charge of the van while handing off a compact sedan to Scott and Nikki.

They returned to the hotel. There was no reason not to, and Scott was in no mood to pick up and run away. Against his better judgment, he needed a few moments to think about what had gone on.

First, he'd lost his team. Second, he had video of John Pike and associates buying chemical weapons. Third, he had John Pike, with no hint of recognition on his face, aiming a gun at him and firing.

He paced the floor as he dialed General Ike on his cell and brought him up to date.

"You need rest, Scott. I can hear the strain in your voice."

"Not now."

"All right. Well, after listening to your version of events, we are left with only two options. Either John Pike has turned, or he's too deep undercover, unofficially undercover as he may be, to explain his actions. These text messages—"

"Every lead he's provided has been a disaster."

"He's never lied to you before. You're suggesting that the man who recruited you into the CIA would construct this elaborate ruse?"

"He did more than train me, sir. You know that."

"What are you really afraid of, Scott?"

Stiletto swallowed, then let out a breath. "I don't know exactly," he said, "but deep down, I'm sure afraid of something."

"Losing your bedrock, maybe?"

"What do you mean?"

"The one sure thing you had, John's guidance and mentorship, when your world was falling apart?"

"Makes as much sense as anything else, General," Stiletto said. He swallowed again. "Maybe you're right."

"It would be the worst loss of all, would it not?"

Stiletto didn't respond.

"Think about how *I* feel, Scott. John Pike and I have known each other longer than you've been alive. When I look at this, I see years of friendship and trust evaporating. I'm just as involved as the two of you."

Stiletto said nothing.

"When we started this mission, you didn't believe John had turned."

Stiletto said, "Then explain how this whole operation is circling the drain."

"I can't explain it, Scott."

"Then tell me what to *do*, General."

"John deserves the benefit of the doubt. You owe him that."

"And our dead agents? Sharke, Reese? What about them?"

It was General Ike Fleming's turn to go quiet. Stiletto listened to the silence on his cell. There was more between them than simply distance, Scott realized.

"It's a tragedy," the general finally said. "They'll be taken care of, of course. As for you, when you catch up with the villains in this scenario, I expect you to dish out your usual brand of justice."

"And if John Pike is guilty?"

"That's up to you, Scott. I can't advise on that."

"You're right. It's not fair to ask, either."

"All I can say is good luck."

Scott and General Ike ended their call. Scott sat on the edge of the bed with his elbows on his knees and his face

in his hands. This was the worst possible outcome. The
only thing he could see left to do, if he ignored General
Ike, was back off and let the CIA handle the problem. Let
the CIA assassins take out John Pike and whoever was
around him, and call an end to this ridiculousness, which
included his own efforts. The smart thing to do was to quit
and call Ali Lewis in San Francisco and say, "Let's give
it another try."

And then a cell phone chimed. Not his personal phone,
the burner phone he'd recovered in San Francisco.

Stiletto moved from the bed to the chair he'd thrown
his jacket over, fishing through the pockets until he found
the burner phone on which Johnny had communicated
earlier. He glanced at the display.

Tell me you're okay.

Scott typed a hurried reply. **You tried to kill me, you
son of a bitch.**

**I'm sorry. I know it looks bad. I'm not a traitor.
Wait for more.**

Stiletto stared at the burner phone for five minutes
before he realized there would be nothing further from
Johnny tonight.

The only thing left to do was call General Ike. Again.
Maybe this time the conversation would be different.

Pike locked the lavatory door and leaned over the sink.
He was afraid he was going to be sick. He had to hold

his elbows close to his body. There wasn't much room to spread without bumping a wall with an elbow. He breathed shallowly.

What a disaster.

How many dead?

Was Scott one of them?

Pike stared into the sink, unable to raise his head to look at his face. He still felt the grime of the asphalt on his hands. There wasn't any blood there, but in his mind's eye, his hands were drenched.

He impulsively clawed for the cell phone in his back pocket and sent a quick text. **Tell me you're okay**.

He leaned against the counter, his eyes locked on the phone for what seemed like an eternity. His pulse rate returned to normal, and he turned to face himself. His face was scuffed a little from rolling into the bushes, but the cuts would heal quickly.

Stay in control. Stay professional. This is what we commit to, the good and the bad. Stay the course. Do not let those deaths go in vain.

And then the phone vibrated.

You tried to kill me, you son of a bitch.

Pike sent his reply and let out a breath. If Scott didn't get the whole story soon, his friend would become his assassin. He had no doubt that Scott, despite his firing from CIA, would advocate that the only person who could take out John Pike was the man who knew him better than anybody, and that was him. Pike flushed the toilet, washed his hands, turned off the light, and stepped back out into the cabin.

But how to tell Scott the story also put everything at risk. He didn't want backup. He didn't want the CIA, Scott Stiletto, or anybody else snooping at his vapor trail because Harrison Joule would sense the surveillance and fade into the wind like he had so many times before.

He returned to the seat near Elsa, the soft leather providing no comfort. She looked at him. "Are you feeling sick?"

"Little shaken."

"We survived."

Pike swallowed as he stared at her. She frowned, and he realized he had been staring for a long time. He should say something about her performance instead of silently hating her.

"That was good shooting."

Her blasting away with two assault weapons like she did it every day had certainly been a sight. He'd almost forgotten what he had been doing at the time—helping Diego load the case into the SUV—before Diego shouted at him to focus.

She smiled, her eyes lighting up with the kind of pride reserved for extravagant acts. "I was trained by the best."

He smiled back but felt no joy. She was a killer. How she had evaded discovery for so many years, he didn't understand. But he'd discovered her now.

He would deal with her soon.

Pike said, "Where is—"

"Right behind you, *mi amigo,*" Diego said, emerging from the galley with two glasses of champagne. "Let's celebrate a successful mission," he said, adding, "In spite of the problems."

Pike accepted the glasses and handed one to Elsa. He watched the bubbles in the champagne race from bottom to top. It was mesmerizing to his scattered mind.

Diego brought out a third glass and rejoined them. He offered a toast, and they clinked glasses and drank. The champagne tasted bitter. Pike drank it down. *He* felt bitter. He wanted to kill both of them, take over the plane, and have the pilots take him straight to Harrison Joule for a final confrontation. He had to end this before any more good guys died.

He lowered the glass with a satisfied exhale instead, smiling at Diego.

"My pleasure to help."

"You'll get your reward soon," Diego said, taking a seat across from them. "The boss takes care of us very well, does he not?"

Elsa agreed and took a long sip of her drink. She eyed Pike hungrily over the rim of her glass.

CHAPTER THIRTY-EIGHT

The jet landed on a small airstrip in what Pike could only call the middle of nowhere.

It wasn't a bad nowhere, with a wide range of rolling hills, all lush green. As he followed Elsa and Diego down the steps to the ground, he said, "Ireland?"

"I figured you'd recognize it."

The Rover bumped along the dirt road, Elsa using the jolts to press her body against Pike. He gave her a look. She smiled and gripped his hand.

Diego, up front, remained quiet.

"Where are we going?" Pike said.

"No idea," said Elsa. "This isn't our headquarters."

"Marco?"

"You'll love it," Diego said. "Let's leave it a surprise."

Pike wanted to say more but held his tongue. He looked out at the rolling countryside, the green hills meeting the blue sky. It was very nice, but only an illusion of peace.

Presently the gray walls of a castle appeared on the

horizon, growing larger as the Rover neared. Diego let out a laugh. "It looks like something from the fifteenth century, but it's actually a modern hotel with all the usual comforts."

Elsa gasped in delight at the sight of the castle appearing to touch the sky. Pike sat stoically, especially when he saw a lone figure standing near the entrance. At the top of a set of crescent-shaped steps stood a man in a white tuxedo jacket, red bow tie, and black slacks.

The Rover rocked to a stop.

Pike didn't move from the back seat right away as Elsa and Diego exited the Rover and started unloading. He stared at the man in the tux. He'd come a long way to meet him, and he wondered what was stopping him from taking out his Browning pistol and killing them all before they set foot inside. First, he didn't know how many troops were around. Second, he didn't know where they had hidden the missiles. It did not make sense to kill the top dog when the instruments of destruction were still in play.

He finally exited the Rover, ignoring a curious look from Elsa, he took his bags and stayed behind Diego as he went up the steps. Diego and the other man greeted each other enthusiastically with hugs and back slaps, and Elsa exchanged a more subdued greeting with the boss. Diego presented Pike with a flourish.

"And this is the new man. A real secret weapon."

"I've heard a lot about you, Mr. Pike. I'm Harrison Joule."

As Pike shook the man's offered hand, a chill crept through his body. He looked into the man's eyes. They weren't dead; they were quite alive, a bright blue, and he wore a Hollywood smile.

"Glad I could be of help," Pike said. "I'm looking forward to the conclusion."

"Wait till you see inside. Come on," Joule said, leading the trio through the front double doors.

The place might have looked like a fifteenth-century castle on the outside, but inside, it was all modern appointment: fixtures, furniture, carpeting, all top-notch. They climbed a circular staircase to the second floor, where their rooms were. Joule made special mention of the room Elsa and Pike would share. Their relationship was not news to him.

"Unpack and get cleaned up," Joule said. "We serve dinner in one hour. The auction starts tomorrow night, so we need to be up early to be on hand when the guests arrive."

Diego said, "How many accepted the invitation?"

"A little more than half. Most of the big money people will be here."

Later, Pike sat quietly while Joule and Diego did most of the talking. He contributed answers to Joule's questions when the big boss finally changed topics, with Elsa adding a few thoughts. Pike's nerves were steady as he went through the motions of dining. There were no thoughts in his head, no question about his next move. He already knew what he had to do. Now all he needed was the proper time.

Diego said, "What about security?"

"I have a few men here already," Joule said, "but tomorrow, the main force arrives. We have mercenaries to keep the place sealed. They're coming over the border. We'll have a small force on the grounds and another patrolling a five-mile radius."

After dinner, Pike and Elsa retired to their room, where they took turns in the shower. Every instinct Pike had told him to lock the door when he took his turn, but he did not. He quickly pulled out his phone and sent Stiletto a text of his approximate location, adding, **Missiles with chemical warheads for sale to highest bidder. Bring plenty of friends.**

He stashed the phone in the pocket of his jeans and stripped for the shower. Ten minutes later, he exited the bathroom wearing a towel.

"About time you got out," Elsa said.

He grinned at her.

She was already naked on the bed, sitting propped up on pillows.

"Stop grinning," she said. "Come to bed."

Pike discarded the towel and followed orders.

A half-hour later, Elsa lay on top of him.

"Have you ever felt trapped?"

Elsa whispered the words, cheek resting on his warm chest. Pike, on his back with one arm behind his head, blinked a few times while he contemplated his answer. He stared at the ceiling. Where was this going?

"Many times," he said. "What do you mean?"

He couldn't see her face in the dark, but he felt her move, her breath on his chest.

"I've only ever worked for Joule," she said.

Pike remained quiet.

Elsa continued, "He saved my life, I guess. I was a teenage orphan in Budapest. My parents were killed in a car wreck, and I wound up on the street. Never mind how."

"Hmmmm."

"I started picking pockets, and one night out in front of a theater, I saw this man. He was tall and handsome, and he looked super-rich. I made a move for his wallet, and I almost got it. He turned and grabbed my wrist. You should have seen his eyes. They looked right through me, almost as if he could see everything inside me."

"He call for the cops?"

"He bought me coffee. We talked for a long time. It was a hypnotic conversation. I told him everything. He said this was no way for me to live, and I should join his organization. He called it the Circle."

"I don't understand what you mean about feeling trapped."

"I'm in love with you, John."

He said, "Oh."

She lifted her head, even though he couldn't see her face. "That's it?"

"I'm surprised."

"Why? Nobody's ever treated me the way you have. You're different. Everything you do is different."

If he didn't play along, she could jeopardize everything. He said, "It's been a long time since—"

"Shhhh. I know. Do you understand?"

"You can't see yourself staying with the Circle, can you?"

She whispered, "No."

"But you feel like you owe Joule, right?"

Another whisper. "Yes."

"Has he said you owe him?"

"Never."

"Has he said you're attached to him forever?"

"No."

"If you tell him you're going with me, you think he'll have a problem?"

"You mean it? You and me?"

"I mean it."

"I know too much," she said.

"We all do. If you were expendable, you wouldn't have lasted this long."

"Are you sure?"

"Trust me, Elsa." He laughed. "I'm older."

"I'm still afraid."

"I don't think you have to be."

"Are you sure?"

"Joule isn't stupid. He'll understand."'

"We'll tell him together?"

"I don't see why not," Pike said.

She let out a sigh and ran her fingers through the hair on his chest.

He felt the walls closing in on him.

Silence descended. Presently, she started to softly snore, but sleep eluded Pike.

What would Elsa do when she realized he was going to kill the man she said had saved her life? There was only one solution: shoot her first.

CHAPTER THIRTY-NINE

Sergei Vasilov of the Russian SVR was the kind of guy who didn't need a driver or a flunky to shout orders at.

He slowed his vehicle at the gate of the castle. Two men in heavy coats, armed with automatic weapons, stood on either side. One held up a hand and approached the car. Vasilov powered down his window and waited for the other man to speak first. The chill in the air wafted into the car. Vasilov was glad for his heavy coat.

"The password, sir."

His chief at SVR continued pushing him to recover Sallig Mahfi's chemical weapon. Fine. Whatever the boss wanted. But not getting usable information out of Morgan Lane had required the SVR to engage in some further legwork.

Via informants, he had learned of the Harrison Joule auction, and Vasilov had put two and two together. A chemical weapon was certainly worth putting up for auction, and the timeline between the events in Berlin,

Austria, and now Ireland made sense. Vasilov had to check it out.

There was no paper invitation to hand over, but instead a password only those who had directly accessed the information would know.

"Crash dive," the Russian said.

The guard waved to his compatriot, who opened the gate. As Vasilov drove through, the dirt beneath his tires crunching a little, two other cars came up the drive behind him. The first guard halted the vehicles as his partner shut the gate once again.

Another armed man in a long coat directed Vasilov to a parking area, where a line of cars already sat. Vasilov stopped his car beside a minivan and killed the engine. As he exited the vehicle, he was struck by the majesty of their surroundings. The rolling green hills created the perfect setting for an out-of-the-way business deal such as this. He would certainly find it relaxing, and he smiled as he lifted the lid of the trunk and took out a single suitcase.

The guard who had directed him gestured toward the front of the hotel and said he would be received inside. As the man turned his attention to the other two incoming cars, Vasilov hoped those inside were a little more hospitable. He wasn't too impressed with the robotic nature of the outside help. Of course, they were hired guns. What could he expect?

He climbed the stone steps to the open double doors, and the warmth inside hit him right away.

A woman behind a podium greeted Vasilov with a bright smile.

"Good afternoon. I'm Elsa," she said. "Your name?"

The Russian gave her his full name. "Sergei Vasilov."

She checked him off a list.

She waved a uniformed attendant over and instructed him to escort Mr. Vasilov to his room. She added, "The dining hall is to the left and down the corridor. Once you're settled, we have drinks and refreshments. Our presentation starts in two hours."

Vasilov said thank you and followed the attendant, who did not offer to take his suitcase. Another hired gun for the occasion. Vasilov decided to stop complaining. He was at an auction for a pair of missiles, not the Ritz-Carlton.

The attendant unlocked the door and stepped back as Vasilov entered, taking the key as he passed the man. The attendant excused himself and walked away. Voices at the other end of the hall caught Vasilov's attention and he turned his head to look, seeing two men he did not recognize, and a third with his back to the Russian who was explaining the evening plans. Vasilov blinked. Something about the third man seemed familiar. He'd seen the back of the man's head somewhere before. The Russian stayed in the doorway long enough to see the man start to turn, and then he was sure. Slipping into his room, Vasilov closed the door. He looked through the peephole as the third man walked by.

The Russian agent smiled. John Pike of the CIA was here. Undercover, or had he suddenly switched from patriot to mercenary? Vasilov figured the former. From what he knew about Pike and their previous dealings, no way would he end up working for somebody like Joule. John Pike would sell shoes at a mall in Kansas first.

The question on his mind was how best to take advantage of the discovery.

Vasilov set his suitcase on the bed and began to unpack.

John Pike went back down the steps to the lobby with a grim set to his face. Pike had only caught a glimpse, but it had been enough. The Russian spymaster was very well-known in the halls of CIA, and while this wasn't like the old days where the removal of such an agent might be discussed, he was certainly not a friend. In this case, he might jeopardize Pike's plan. He would either have to work out an alliance with the Russian and help him with what he obviously wanted, the missiles, or kill him.

With another murder on his mind, Pike entered the lobby and saw Elsa at the front, greeting more guests. They were arriving all at once, which gave him a chance to record names and faces in his head for later filing purposes. Some of the guests had been on the wanted list for a long time. If he could learn anything about them while accomplishing his personal mission, so much the better. The extra intelligence might keep him off the chopping block.

He rejoined Elsa at the front and prepared for the next batch of arrivals.

CHAPTER FORTY

Scott Stiletto read John Pike's text over the phone to General Ike.

"What do you make of it?" the general said.

"Let's put the pieces of what we have together and see if it adds up," Stiletto said. They went down the sequence of events, starting with San Francisco and Oscar DeSoto, the confrontation off the coast of Greece with James Fox, and the information he'd provided, and finally, the chemical weapons sold by Morgan Lane to John Pike's party.

The general said, "Here's how I see it. John Pike, for some reason, abandoned his post to join this crew collecting missile parts from around the world. Now those parts are assembled and the missiles are for sale, and he's given us the location of the purchase point."

"I agree."

"I can have you and Nikki Fortune on a plane to Ireland within an hour, but you certainly can't go in alone."

"I'm open to suggestions."

"This is the sort of thing the locals might want a crack at, so I will alert our opposites in Ireland and see if we can put something together. Pack your bags."

Stiletto and Nikki left Austria very quickly, boarding a chartered jet to Ireland and linking up with Irish secret service representatives upon landing. From there, meetings were brief. The Irish didn't want weapons of mass destruction moving through their territory any more than anybody else did, so they assembled a strike plan that included Stiletto and Nikki.

Thirty volunteers of the Army Ranger Wing, the Irish Special Forces otherwise known as the SFA, joined the raiding party. They had a simple plan: hit the location John Pike had provided, recover the chemical weapons reportedly on the grounds, and take no prisoners.

Stiletto and Nikki met with the major leading the operation and hitched a ride in his AgustaWestland AW139 helicopters to fulfill their part of the mission: the recovery of a CIA asset.

The chopper contained the fifteen of them, complete with their rifles and equipment. The SFA troops were decked out in green with dark berets, their weapons between their knees. Stiletto sat near a window in the very back, watching the green countryside as the sun set and wishing he was there for another reason. Nikki sat next to him. The seats were thin, basically metal frames with canvas inserts, and not terribly comfortable. They sat very close together.

The rest of the cabin was bare of anything non-essential to allow more room for gear. A second chopper similarly loaded stayed a little behind the first.

The sky began to darken quickly as the sun dropped behind the far mountains.

The chopper dipped and started for the ground. The pilot announced they'd be landing in two minutes.

"You ready?" Nikki said.

Stiletto turned to face her. "More than I thought I would be."

"Good. So am I."

The chopper touched down with a short jolt.

Joule stood and tapped a wine glass with a fork. The ringing echoed through the dining hall, and the mutterings of the guests faded to silence.

He and Diego occupied the head table at the front of the hall; Pike and Elsa were at another table off to the side. The troops from outside were now inside, although their automatic rifles had been traded for sidearms. Joule addressed his guests, the threat of any kind of violence far from his mind.

Close to one hundred faces looked back at him, some turning their chairs so they could see him. They waited patiently, the partial remains of dinner on some plates, while others were clean. The servers had vacated as soon as Joule stood. There would be no serving of any kind while he spoke.

"I suppose you wonder why I've called you here to-day," he said with a smile.

The audience laughed.

"I appreciate you all taking the time to attend our auction. As you know, we have quite a product to display. My people and I have assembled a pair of missiles tipped with a chemical weapon assembled by a former ISIS scientist named Sallig Mahfi."

Muted gasps filled the hall.

"The highest bidder takes it home."

Somebody called, "Where is it?"

"Funny you should ask," Joule said as the hall doors opened and two guards wheeled in a cart supporting a flatscreen television, the screen at least sixty inches. They stopped beside the head table. Joule turned the screen on with a remote control taken from his pocket. The picture appeared, showing both missiles in a gray-walled room. They sat in a foam-lined steel case.

"The missiles are safely off-site, and this is a live feed from their location."

More murmurs filled the hall. Joule paid them no mind. Somebody in the back raised his hand. Joule asked everybody to quiet down and called on the man. "Your question, Mr. Vasilov?"

"How do we know this is truly a live feed?" the Russian said.

"I have a man behind the camera who will follow any

direction you give to prove he is live. As many as who would like to speak to my man are welcome to come up." Joule held out a phone.

Only six of the guests started forward, although some started to rise and sat down again when they saw how many were already going up. Joule let each man use his phone in turn, and the requests ranged from asking the camera operator to show ten fingers or do jumping jacks to sticking a finger in his ear. The camera operator complied with each one. Joule took his phone back as the last man returned to his table, thanked the operator, and killed the connection.

"Any other questions?"

Somebody said, "If we win, do we take delivery tonight?"

"The winner of the auction," Joule said, "will designate where he wants the missiles delivered, and my people will have them at your preferred destination within twenty-four hours."

Joule again asked for questions, but this time there were none.

"Shall we start the bidding at ten million US?"

Pike covered his concern with a sip of coffee.

As the cameraman went through the requested motions, all he could think was that the missiles weren't in the building.

Now what?

He'd had no indication that the missiles were off-site. They could be down in the basement for all he knew, and Joule was using the video feed as a way to fool the guests into giving up any plans of stealing them.

Pike took a deep breath as he felt Elsa's hand on his leg. He smiled at her. The video changed nothing. He wore the Browning nine-millimeter under his dinner jacket and had several spare magazines in his pockets.

He had not come this far to change the plan.

The bidding continued briskly. Elsa paid more attention to Pike than the action around her. She still needed to talk to Joule about her desire to leave, but watching John and tracing the lines of his jaw with her eyes filled her with the kind of confidence she felt emanating from him.

As the dollar amount climbed above eleven million, she looked out at the faces of the guests and squeezed Pike's leg a little harder than she'd intended to.

"What is it?"

"Those two who just got up."

Pike followed her gaze. The pair slipped through the doors of the dining hall and closed them quietly.

"They probably think the missiles are in the basement or something," Pike said.

"We can't let them wander around."

"Stay here. I'll go explain it to them."

Pike wiped his mouth and left the table.

Elsa watched him go and glanced at Joule as he continued to encourage bidders. Twelve million dollars.

"Do I hear 12.5?" Joule asked. "Twelve-point-five million dollars?"

If Elsa had kept her eyes on Pike, she'd have seen Sergei Vasilov leave his table and follow him.

CHAPTER FORTY-ONE

The low lights on the walls let Pike see the two men as they moved down the length of the hall, checking doors and talking quietly, obviously looking for some sort of access to the basement. Pike didn't even know if there was a basement, so they were probably wasting their time. But if they were looking for the missiles, they had something in mind other than paying for them.

Pike took out the nine-millimeter, and from the pocket of his slacks he removed a silencer, which he screwed onto the end of the barrel. He started down the hall as the pair found a door and pushed through. They stopped midway through and conferred briefly, then went all the way in and shut the door. Pike quickened his steps. He paused at the door for a moment, then pivoted with the Browning at arm's length. The snout of the silencer stopped an inch from Vasilov's face.

"Took you long enough, Mr. Pike."

Pike lowered the gun. "We can't talk here." He popped

the door open. "Step into my office."

Pike stepped through the door, and Vasilov followed. The door clicked shut.

"Aren't you looking for somebody?" the Russian said.

"I know where they're going. The question is whether I leave you down there with them."

Vasilov held up both hands. "I'm sure you had a graceful exit from the CIA and have found a good job here, right?"

"Sure."

"Unless you'd hate for me to say something to Mr. Joule about your illustrious career."

"Why would I hate for you to do that?"

"He wouldn't like having an undercover agent at his party."

"If I was undercover, would this auction be happening right now?"

"Not if the missiles weren't here."

"What are you doing here, Vasilov?"

"My country wants the missiles."

"Buy them."

"Why buy when you can steal?"

"You aren't stealing anything, Sergei."

Vasilov's face softened. Pike frowned.

"What's really on your mind?" the American said.

The Russian shook his head. "You know as well as I do why Moscow wants this weapon. They're going to put it into inventory and use it. Someday."

"You want to make sure it's destroyed?"

"The thought had occurred to me."

"The man in charge of this thing," Pike said, "killed my wife."

"I understand."

"We can help each other."

"Indeed."

"Nobody would ever have to know."

"I concur," the Russian said.

Pike extended his hand. Vasilov accepted it. The two men shook.

Pike let Vasilov go first and they started down a set of steps, turned left at the landing, and stepped into a hallway with a bright light in the center of the room.

They surprised the two men in the room, who stood there incredulously.

The room was empty of anything resembling the missiles.

"What are you doing here?" Pike said.

One of the two came forward half a step, an Asian with thick black hair slicked across the top, his chiseled jawline leading to a line of stitches on his chin. The man stopped short when Pike raised the silenced Browning. Pike sensed Vasilov moving to his right side. He also produced a pistol, a compact Makarov.

"We're looking for the missiles," Stitches said. "Obviously they are not here."

The second man, another Asian, the extra padding

around the middle not concealed by his open windbreaker, stepped back.

"Neither of you moves again," Pike said. "Are we not treating you well? Why are you causing trouble?"

"The missiles are not here, and this auction is a fraud," Stitches said. "I will tell everybody and end this obvious attempt to extort our money."

Stitches lifted his foot.

"Not another move," Pike warned.

Stitches lowered his foot.

Pike shot in him in the chest.

The bullet hit Stitches high and he choked as he fell back, Thick Middle shifting to avoid the falling body. Thick Middle's eyes were wide, his mouth open and his left hand clawing for a gun, but he had trouble drawing. Pike didn't think he was much of a shooter, probably a bomb expert who could examine the missiles. He fired a second shot that punched through the bridge of Thick Middle's nose.

Only the thuds of the falling bodies and the click of the Browning's action made any noise, and a pungent cloud of cordite hung in the air as Pike pivoted to face Vasilov with his aim steady.

The Russian held up his hands, then carefully placed his pistol on the ground and moved back.

"No need, John. We have a deal."

Pike lowered his weapon.

"Our countries might be rivals in the recent global tensions," Vasilov began, "and we've been rivals in the past, but that doesn't mean we can't work together. I know what you're going through, John."

"Nobody else is going to get hurt by anything with Joule's fingerprints on it," Pike stated, "and nobody is going to stop me."

"I'm not going to betray you."

Pike put away his gun.

"All right, Sergei, here's what we do…"

Pike came back into the upstairs hallway and bumped into Elsa and Diego.

"Everything okay, *mi amigo*?"

"We had a situation," Pike said. "Some of our guests thought the missiles were downstairs and confessed to wanting to steal them. They won't bother us again."

Elsa let out a sigh.

Diego slapped Pike on the arm. "Good work. The auction's getting hot; we should get back."

"The bodies—"

"Details, details, *mi amigo*." Diego laughed. "Let somebody else worry about the details. Let's get back to the party."

Elsa smiled. Pike didn't argue.

There was applause in the dining hall as Pike, Elsa, and

Diego entered. The winning bid had come in at an even twenty million US. Joule announced he would meet personally with the winner to arrange delivery details; meanwhile, everyone was to make themselves at home and enjoy the food and drink provided.

Pike, back at his table with Elsa, checked his watch after a while. "Maybe we should call it a night."

"Night's still young," she said.

"I know." He winked.

She smiled. "Let's go."

They cut through the crowd and took the elevator to their floor.

As Pike shut the door, Elsa scooted into the bathroom for a moment. He crossed the room to the window, the sky dark enough so he could see his partial reflection in the glass. He avoided looking directly into his face. He didn't want to see what was there.

There was movement in the distance beyond the walls of the property. Pike instinctively stepped to the side of the window frame, peeking out along the edge. Was his mind playing tricks on him? It didn't look like anything was out there at second glance.

He pulled the curtains shut as the toilet flushed. Elsa said something Pike didn't hear because he was more concerned with the sudden gunfire and the string of explosions from outside that rocked the building.

CHAPTER FORTY-TWO

"We have strict orders not to destroy the building," the SFA colonel said.

Stiletto gave him a funny look he probably couldn't see in the dark. "So why the mortars?"

A line of troops had three launchers set up behind a small hill, their scopes set on the castle.

"For the cars," the colonel said. "We don't want anybody getting away, right?" He smiled.

Stiletto looked at Nikki Fortune, who either wasn't listening or didn't care as she examined their objective through night-vision binoculars. She said, "A lot of light on the ground floor, but the windows are covered."

The SFA colonel, whose name was Sean Gallagher, checked in with his squad leaders through the wireless radio in his ear. He, Stiletto, Nikki, and the mortar team were approximately fifty yards from the castle behind a rise. The rest of the SFA troops were spread out in attack position, ready to pounce as soon as the mortars dropped.

Stiletto and Nikki, outfitted with the same kit and armaments as the attack squads, would start their advance after the main fight commenced. The goal of the attack force was to engage Joule's troops and keep them occupied while they infiltrated to find John Pike.

No turning back now. Stiletto had no intention of walking out of there without his friend, one way or another.

It was the "another" part that bothered him the most.

Gallagher gave the order, and the first mortars belched from the launch tubes.

The shells exploded in the parking area, two cars going up in balls of flame. The explosions spread to neighboring cars and ignited them as well, so the night sky lit up almost like day. The attack squads moved in, flame licking from the barrels of their automatic weapons as they fired at the troops rushing out of the building.

The mortar tubes belched again, the shells dropping on target. The rest of the cars parked in front of the castle burst into flames.

"Go!" Colonel Gallagher shouted. He leaped over the rise, with Stiletto and Nikki close behind them. Scott's lungs started to burn with exertion as they cleared twenty-five yards and reached the broken spot in the wall where the strike force had penetrated. Gunfire cracked through the grounds, and more gunfire on the inside told them the fight had spread there as well.

Stiletto and Nikki dived through the shattered window of the dining hall and rolled left into the cover of an overturned table, plates and leftover food scattered all around them. Bullets *thwacked* into the wood as they dropped flat, a crack appearing from top to bottom. The table did not split, however.

Stiletto fired a burst around the side, driving a green-coated gunman to cover, then surveyed the scene.

Food scraps all over, men down and bleeding, some not moving at all. Tables overturned, white tablecloths cast aside like so much rubbish. Most of the fighting was out in the main hall. Two green coats broke for the exit, staying low and moving fast around the obstacles. Stiletto and Nikki swung up their weapons and fired, taking both gunners down. Stiletto broke cover and started checking bodies, but she found no sign of Pike.

Nikki stopped as they reached the exit.

"Ready?" she said.

"Let's go!"

They both ran out into the hall with their weapons tight to their shoulders.

"We have to— *John!*"

"Stay where you are, Elsa."

"Why are you pointing a gun at me?"

He wasn't so much as pointing the Browning at *her* as he was aiming for her right eye.

"I'm not who I said I am, Elsa."

She started to shake. "What?"

"I'm a CIA agent. Joule killed my wife. A long time ago in Paris."

"You used me!" It wasn't a question.

"Perfectly."

A red flush crawled up her neck, but before Elsa said anything more, the Browning spat once.

It took a lot of willpower not to look at her body as he stepped around her. He slipped out into the hall. The gunfire from the first floor wasn't letting up.

Backup had finally arrived.

Pike stalked down the hall with his eyes fixed ahead.

Your time is up, Joule.

Movement around the corner. Pike brought up the Browning but held his fire as Sergei Vasilov approached with his gun up.

"It's me," he said.

"Let's go," Pike said.

Pike found a stairwell and moved cautiously up the steps, with the Russian behind him. Assuming Joule had escaped the dining hall when the first explosions hit-and it wasn't impossible—he'd go to his room to gather anything important before escaping. Or trying to. They were out in the open, vehicles destroyed, and surrounded by troops. Getting away wasn't going to be easy, and Pike had another problem. He was not identifiable as a good guy. Unless Scott found him, he could be shot by his own people.

Having Vasilov with him might help. Scott might recognize the SVR operative too.

As he climbed the steps, he didn't feel much like a good guy.

He and Vasilov reached the next floor, paused to look, and advanced at a brisk clip.

"Who's attacking?" Vasilov said.

"Hopefully, friends," Pike said.

The gunfire seemed to have slackened. Had the cavalry subdued the enemy? He stopped at the half-open doorway of Joule's room and heard movement inside. He pushed the door open and let the Browning lead the way. Vasilov followed behind with his own pistol up in a two-hand grip.

"Harrison."

"Oh, thank goodness," Joule said. "Help me with this other case. What are you doing? Who is this with you?"

Joule stood at a table. He was loading his laptop into a briefcase, another case with papers to the side. His eyes were locked on Pike's Browning pistol as if he had never seen a gun before.

"Paris. 1983. You set off a bomb and killed my wife and my unborn child."

Joule tuned white.

"I came here to kill you."

Pike's finger tightened on the trigger.

"Not so fast, *mi amigo*."

Vasilov spun to shoot the new arrival but didn't complete the trigger pull. Diego shot him twice. As the Russian fell, Pike didn't hesitate. There were a couch and coffee table slightly to his left. He bolted, stepped onto the table, and launched over the back of the couch. Diego's gun cracked behind him and the shots split the air as he landed hard on the other side of the couch, the impact sending a jolt of pain through his body. He let out a cry and rolled onto his back, the Browning coming up as Diego approached from around the other side of the couch. Pike fired once. Diego's head snapped back, and he hit the floor like a puppet with its strings cut. As Pike struggled to get up, Joule dove for Diego's gun and grabbed it, the pistol almost slipping from his hand. He got a grip and swung the sights on Pike, but the CIA agent fired first; the shot followed the line of Joule's extended arm and struck below the shoulder. Joule cried out and dropped the gun, collapsing to curl into a ball.

The gun landed a foot away from Joule. He started to drag himself toward it as Pike breathlessly gained his feet. Gasping, he walked over and kicked the gun away, then stepped on Joule's hand. Joule winced. He looked up into the snout of the Browning.

"You ready?" Pike said.

"Quit talking and do it already."

The shot pinned Joule's head to the carpet.

Pike staggered back, landing in a chair.

He sat there and stared at Joule's body, his eyes rising to the briefcases on the table. Maybe the information therein would tell where the missiles were and identify any associates. He frowned. Had he forgotten about the body already? He looked at the man he'd traveled so far and been through so much to kill, but he didn't feel any sense of accomplishment.

He looked at Vasilov's body on the floor. Sudden violence was part of Pike's life. Part of Vasilov's too, and the Russian had finally reached a moment where he hadn't been fast enough.

But he'd been there when it counted. In a way, he'd saved Pike's life.

At a cost Pike would carry for the rest of his life.

"Sorry, Sergei," he said.

Stiletto and Nikki checked doors along the hall. Some were unlocked and they did a quick recon of those rooms, finding nobody. On to the next, all the way down the hall until they came to an open door.

Scott held up a fist of caution as they approached, and he stopped near the doorway and glanced in. He waved her around and Nikki entered first, weapon ready, then lowered it with a cry as she saw the man collapsed in the chair.

"John!"

Stiletto rushed to him. John Pike looked up. His face showed a tiredness Stiletto had never seen before. Scott knelt in front of the older man. "You all right?"

Pike nodded. "I'm fine now. I'm glad you found me."

John Pike looked beaten and worn out, but the pistol clutched in his hand and the bodies on the carpet said otherwise. Scott's eyes landed on the Russian.

"Vasilov?"

Pike nodded.

"He was with you on this?"

"For a few minutes." Pike paused for a moment, then, "I'm glad you found me."

"We've been checking rooms—"

Pike raised his gun. He pointed it past Stiletto at one of the men on the floor. "Him."

Stiletto turned to look at Harrison Joule's body but had no comprehension of what Pike meant.

"He killed my wife and daughter. Paris. All those years ago."

Stiletto said, "Is that what this was all about?"

Pike nodded.

"We gotta get you out of here, Johnny."

"Hallway's clear," Nikki Fortune said, standing near the doorway, her eyes and weapon pointed the way they had come.

"Get the briefcases," Pike said, rising to his full height. He stretched and groaned.

Stiletto slung his weapon and took Joule's briefcases in each hand.

"I'm not a kid anymore," Pike said. "Lead the way,

Scotty."

Colonel Gallagher and his SFA team secured the site, rounded up survivors, and called for transport vehicles to carry the prisoners away. Stiletto, Nikki, and John Pike sat far from the activity on the cold grass, waiting for a helicopter to come and collect them. Pike told his story in as much detail as he could, omitting nothing of what he knew of William Strong's murder and the shootout in Austria.

When he finished, nobody said anything. The cool night air had dried the sweat on their faces, the battle finally behind them—not only the battle at the castle, but the battle for the crimes of the past as well.

Tomorrow would take care of itself.

CHAPTER FORTY-THREE

Scott Stiletto let out a laugh as he parked beside the Starbucks on Old Dominion Drive in McLean, Virginia. John Pike had wanted to meet and tell him about the CIA's decision regarding his future. Scott figured he already knew the answer, but he wanted to hear it from Pike's mouth in case he was wrong.

What he saw through the window made his head hurt. It looked like half the staff of Clandestine Operations was inside. He recognized many faces.

The Starbucks was close to CIA headquarters, and CIA employees were lazy enough that if they wanted to meet off-campus, it took less effort to visit the Starbucks than find somewhere else.

Thus, many CIA agents ended up at this particular coffee shop. Scott was amazed that the Agency kept anything secret or accomplished any goal whatsoever. And the laziness probably explained more than a few public failures. The funny part was watching them ignore each other while pretending they weren't violating serious procedural rules.

He shook his head, exited the car, and walked around to the front, where he found John Pike waiting.

He handed Scott a cup. "It's green tea."

Stiletto took a sip. It was hot. "Thanks."

"Idiots inside. You should have seen them all try not to choke when they saw me. I think the verdict has gotten around."

Stiletto didn't ask what the verdict was.

"Let's take a walk," Pike said.

They started along the sidewalk. There were no other pedestrians, but plenty of traffic.

Stiletto glanced nervously at Pike. Two days earlier, he had testified at Pike's disciplinary hearing, explaining what he had learned during the chase and how Pike's actions had undoubtedly saved many lives and taken out plenty of bad guys as a bonus.

It had felt weird being back in the building with a guest badge and a security escort, but his friend needed him. He wasn't going to tell him no or let mixed emotions about returning to the Agency keep him away.

"I appreciate everything you told them," Pike said.

"I had to," Scott said. "You needed me like I needed you once."

Pike smiled. "Still no contact with Felicia?"

"We aren't talking about my daughter today, John."

"All right."

"What did the committee say?"

Pike shrugged. "I'm out on my ass. They'll let me keep my retirement package."

"I figured. At least you got retirement. I lost all mine." Stiletto cursed. The discipline committees never seemed to waver on their enforcement of CIA policy despite evidence that maybe they should take it easy sometimes.

"If you want, John," Scott said, "you can come and work with me at the Trust."

"I thought I'd go fishing instead."

"Fishing is good too."

"It's time I quit anyway," he said. "I think I've taken all the chances I'm allowed. If I get tangled in something else, I probably won't make it next time."

"Don't talk like that."

"Fact of life, Scott. You can only get away with so much before it catches up with you."

"Is that a message?"

"It's a lesson," Pike said, "based on hard-earned experience."

They paused at a crosswalk. Traffic continued around them, nobody aware of the drama playing out in the lives of the two men.

"Felicia still not talking to you?"

Stiletto frowned.

"We're done talking about me, Scott."

"I suppose we are."

"So?"

"We are still not communicating."

Pike sighed. The light changed, and they crossed the street to continue walking.

"I wish there was a magic formula to give you to change that," Pike said.

"Uh-huh."

"Maybe she'll come around someday."

"There might not be many somedays left, according to your philosophy."

"Then maybe you have some decisions to make."

"What does that mean?" *Although I think I know.*

"Maybe if you tell her you're coming fishing with me, she'll be open to communicating."

"You're assuming that's her reason, John. You don't *know* what her reason is. Or has she told you?"

"No, she hasn't told me."

Stiletto swallowed some tea as he mentally counted to ten. Yelling at Pike wasn't going to solve anything.

"I didn't mean to upset you," Pike said.

"It's okay."

"You need to consider the future. Seriously."

"I know. I'm not ready."

"Time's running out for us all, Scott. It's time to get serious."

"Are you done?"

Pike nodded. "Yeah, I'm done."

Stiletto watched Pike drive out of the Starbucks parking lot, gave a final wave, and climbed into his car. He adjusted the rearview mirror to see his face. He stared at himself long enough to realize he might look like an idiot to somebody passing, so he put the mirror back in place, started the car, and drove away.

Pike was making him ask the same question Ali Lewis had posed in San Francisco several months ago, and he still didn't know the answer.

Yes, he thought he should step away from the action and call it a career.

No, he didn't want to.

Both answers were right, depending on the day and time.

His cell phone rang. Scott peeked at the display and quickly pulled over to answer.

"Hi, Nikki."

"Am I calling at a bad time?"

"No, what's up?"

"I was thinking that since I helped get your buns out of the fire, maybe you could return the favor."

"What's happening?"

"Those gun thugs I mentioned to you are still after me for shooting their boss. Want to help me take the fight to them?"

"Are you still in the States?"

"Yeah, the Watergate. I love this hotel. So much history!"

Stiletto laughed. Yes, he'd return the favor. Yes, he'd get back into action. Damn the torpedoes.

Because Pike was wrong.

There was still plenty of time. What mattered was how he used what time was allotted to him.

"I'm twenty minutes away," he said.

"See you soon."

Scott Stiletto put the phone away and steered back into traffic.

IF YOU LIKED THIS BOOK, CHECK OUT THE DANGEROUS MR. WOLF

MR. WOLF IS A BRAND-NEW HERO THAT YOU CAN ROOT FOR FROM THE AUTHOR OF THE HARD-EDGED SCOTT STILETTO THRILLERS – BRIAN DRAKE.

When innocent people are in the crossfire and the police are unable to help, Wolf picks up where the law leaves off.

As he hunts for clues through the city's dark alleys, chasing mafia killers, solving a decades-old crime, or helping a widow unravel the mystery behind a murder attempt, he quickly uncovers the hidden hands behind the violence, but even he isn't ready for the shocking twists when the last bullets are fired.

THE DANGEROUS MR. WOLF is your introduction to a good man to have on your side.

Better pray he stays there.

AVAILABLE NOW ON AMAZON

ABOUT THE AUTHOR

A twenty-five year veteran of radio and television broad-casting, Brian Drake has spent his career in San Francisco where he's filled writing, producing, and reporting duties with stations such as KPIX-TV, KCBS, KQED, among many others. Currently carrying out sports and traffic reporting duties for Bloomberg 960, Brian Drake spends time between reports and carefully guarded morning and evening hours cranking out action/adventure tales.

Brian Drake lives in California with his wife and two cats, and when he's not writing he is usually blasting along the back roads in his Corvette with his wife telling him not to drive so fast, but the engine is so loud he usu-ally can't hear her.

You will find him regularly blogging at:
www.briandrake88.blogspot.com

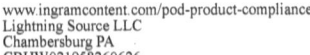